The Hours After Midnight...

The Hours After Midnight...

Tales of Terror
and the Supernatural by
J. Sheridan Le Fanu

Edited and with an Introduction by
DES HICKEY

Illustrations by **GEOFFREY BOURNE-TAYLOR**

Leslie Frewin of London

First published 1975 by
Leslie Frewin Publishers Limited,
Five Goodwin's Court,
Saint Martin's Lane,
London WC2N 4LL, England.

This book is set in Garamond Bold
Photoset, printed and bound in Great Britain by
Weatherby Woolnough, Sanders Road,
Wellingborough, Northamptonshire

ISBN 0 85632 144 3

Contents

Illustrations

Introduction
Le Fanu, the 'Invisible Prince'

A HOUSE GUEST in a story by Henry James finds a volume of Sheridan Le Fanu by his bedside, 'ideal reading in a country house for the hours after midnight'. The guest has just arrived, but, in Jamesian fashion, he dips into the book straight away and in consequence is late for dinner.

The incident would have amused Sheridan Le Fanu, who wrote primarily with the intention of telling a good story and sometimes introduced a narrator who urged the reader to draw his chair nearer the fire as the storm rattled the windows and the wind whispered hoarsely among the chimney pots and the limbs of the old trees. Like the master storyteller he was, Le Fanu was determined that his readers should feel cosily apprehensive before he unleashed his terrors; 'a premonitory chilling of the blood' was how Nelson Browne, who has written the fullest study of Le Fanu, described the opening of *Dickon the Devil*. As Herbert van Thal suggested when he reprinted *Madam Crowl's Ghost:* 'Read it – as all such stories should be read – in the silence of the night in a lonely house; it will not fail to keep its victim uneasily afraid of putting out the light and admitting the terrifying shadows of a night peopled by Le Fanu's haunted imagination.'

When another James, M R James, introduced the almost forgotten Le Fanu to twentieth century readers in 1923 with a collection of lost or neglected stories, he remarked: 'Nobody sets the scene better than he; nobody touches in the effective detail more deftly.' Le Fanu stood for James 'absolutely in the front rank as a writer of ghost stories'. This was his deliberate verdict after reading all the supernatural tales he could lay his hands on.

Le Fanu's decline in popularity after the turn of the century is as undeniable as his own lack of success with his first two novels, a failure which discouraged him as a writer of fiction for more than fifteen years. But when he got into his stride again he became a mid-Victorian favourite as a writer of tales of terror and the supernatural. In Ireland he is claimed as an Irish writer. The tall, dark house in which he died a death as bizarre as any in his own pages has been endowed with a commemorative plaque. But Le Fanu was caught, as many Anglo-Irishmen are, in a tug of loyalties between Anglo-Saxon and Gaelic cultures. Like another Anglo-Irish writer of the Gothic, Charles Maturin, who probably influenced him, Le Fanu was of Huguenot descent. His family tree has been traced to 1536 when a Michel Le Fanu took his degree in arts at the University of Caen, and then went on to study law and write poetry. Three hundred years later Sheridan Le Fanu was also to take his degree, study law and write poetry. Michel's only son Etienne was also a poet and a lawyer, and Etienne's son Pierre bought the *fief noble* of Cresserons, near Caen, so that his successors became entitled to call themselves Seigneurs de Cresserons. When Sheridan Le Fanu first published *The House by the Churchyard* in serial form he used the pseudonym Charles de Cresserons.

A Charles Le Fanu de Cresserons was one of the refugee Huguenots fleeing from religious persecution in France before the Revolution. He joined the army of William of Orange in Holland, fought as a captain in the Irish campaign and decided to settle in Dublin in 1710. In Ireland, as in England, the Le Fanus prospered. Joseph Sheridan Le Fanu was born in Dublin on 28th August 1814, to Thomas Philip Le Fanu, the curate of a city church, and his wife Emma. His sister Catherine had been born a year earlier and his brother William was born two years later. William Le Fanu described their childhood days in his autobiography *Seventy Years of Irish Life*. The earliest days were at Chapelizod, a rustic Dublin suburb where Thomas Le Fanu was chaplain to the military school in the nearby Phoenix Park. Chapelizod became the setting for *The House by the Churchyard* and a number of short stories, one of which is included in this collection. Later the family moved to Abington in the south, near Limerick, where the father was rector. Even in those days young Joseph, though a practical joker, was inclined to solitude. He had a hideaway in the roof of the rectory to which he would retreat when visitors called. He also wrote poetry as a boy which he showed only to his mother and his sister and brother. His schooling seems to have taken place in his father's well-stocked library; even when he and his brother became un-dergraduates at Trinity College in Dublin they were excused lectures because they were 'on the country lists' and so travelled to Dublin only for the university examinations.

Joseph Sheridan Le Fanu took his degree in 1837 and was called to the Bar two years later. But in 1838 he had had his first story published in the *Dublin*

12

University Magazine (which had no connection with the university other than having been founded by Trinity men) and this may have been one reason why his career took an unpredictable turn. At the university he had won a medal for oratory and been President of the College Historical Society; naturally his friends predicted a brilliant career for him at the Bar. Instead, he turned to journalism, bought and edited a newspaper, *The Warden*, and later bought two more newspapers and merged all three as the Dublin *Evening Mail*, which was to survive until the middle of this century. To his brother William these ventures were 'injurious to his future prospects, as they prevented him from applying himself to a profession for which eloquence and a ready wit acquitted him, and of which his contemporaries had hoped to see him a distinguished member.'

Le Fanu never practised as a barrister. He ran his papers by day and wrote fiction by night. Even when he had become a recluse in the years before his death he continued his habit of writing late into the night. He was a case study in Anglo-Irish versatility.

But it soon became apparent to Le Fanu that he wasn't making his name as a writer. All his early stories written for the *Dublin University Magazine* and later collected in three volumes under the title *The Purcell Papers* were set in Ireland, with the exception of *Schalken the Painter*. His first novels, *The Cock and Anchor* and *The Fortunes of Torlough O'Brien*, which had Irish backgrounds, were unsuccessful. Le Fanu must have been depressed; more so when he knew that his friends were contrasting his apparent failure

13

with the achievements of his college rivals. In an introduction to an edition of Le Fanu's *Uncle Silas* Elizabeth Bowen expressed surprise that the novel should have an English setting; she found Le Fanu's reason for transferring what seemed to her an Irish story to the English countryside 'inscrutable'. An American critic, Michael H Begnal, has decided that Le Fanu's work becomes clearer when transposed to an Irish setting. To Begnal Le Fanu's London is really Dublin and his English mansions are the Irish 'big houses' of the period. Though no one has said so, I would have thought that Le Fanu wanted his work to be popular and soon realised that his market lay with that large body of readers across the Irish Sea. Not only did he begin to give his characters English names and place them in English settings, but he abandoned his early ambition to be an Irish Walter Scott.

In 1844 Le Fanu married the daughter of a QC, Susan Bennett, by whom he had two sons and two daughters. One of his sons, Brinsley, became an artist and was to illustrate a novel and a collection of stories by his father in the 1890s. In 1858 Le Fanu's wife died prematurely and the author gradually became a recluse in the house at 70 Merrion Square which his wife had inherited on the death of her father in 1851. Previously they had lived for a few years first at number 1 and then at number 15 Warrington Place, a street's length away from Merrion Square on the banks of the Grand Canal. These were neat Georgian houses; number 1 has been replaced by an office block and number 15 is not likely to survive the developer, but the house in Merrion Square, today the headquarters of the Irish Arts Council, is much as it must have looked in Le Fanu's time. It is a large and splendid house on the south side of one of Europe's largest squares, but the tall fronts of the houses on this side of the square seldom catch the sun. The lofty hall leads to a surprisingly wide staircase. On the first floor the three windows of the drawing room overlooking the trees and lawns of the square reach almost'from ceiling to floor. On the ground floor the room which Le Fanu used as a study has a deep bay window overlooking a narrow garden with a coach-house at the rear. The garden is hidden from its neighbours by tall brick walls which give it a cloistered atmosphere. It was here that Le Fanu walked on fine days, filling his pockets with pebbles and dropping them one at a time at each end of the garden until his pockets were empty; he would then return to his study where he sat at a desk which had belonged to the playwright Richard Brinsley Sheridan, his grand-uncle. At night he wrote in bed by the light of two wax candles, keeping warm in winter with a fire in the Adam fireplace. Around midnight he would extinguish the candles and sleep for a couple of hours. Then he would waken and write again, propping his notebook on his knees, until early dawn, and then sleep again, not leaving his bedroom until noon. His withdrawal from society was gradual; he had been sociable enough after his wife's death and continued to visit his newspaper office and edit the *Dublin University Magazine.* which he had purchased in 1861, succeeding Charles Lever

15

as editor (he finally disposed of the magazine in 1869). On his way home to Merrion Square he would slip into a bookshop in search of works on the supernatural. He read deeply in Swedenborg, as his later stories show, and became quite death-haunted in his last years. Dublin, always good with nicknames, called him the 'Invisible Prince'. Towards the end he lived in isolation. He saw his immediate family, but seldom his friends. Even his good friend Lever was turned from his door on his last visit to Dublin.

T P Le Fanu, in a privately-printed history of the Le Fanu family in 1924, compared him to one of his fictional characters, Austin Ruthyn in *Uncle Silas.* Ruthyn's wife dies young and he withdraws into seclusion. 'This bereavement, I have been told, changed him, made him more odd and taciturn than ever. He ultimately became, I am told, a Swedenborgian.' At least Austin Ruthyn didn't brew strong tea over a spirit lamp in the middle of the night, as Le Fanu used to do.

Le Fanu had shown a morbid temperament in his earliest stories, a temperament that may have been influenced by the death of his sister, probably from the ubiquitous consumption, at the age of twenty-seven. His wife's death increased his morbidity, and the dark house in Merrion Square, the heavily-draped bedroom in which Le Fanu wrote and the endless cups of tea which gave him nightmares cannot have made his nature any less gloomy.

His nightmares provided material for his stories, but they finally got the better of him. Frequently he dreamed of a crumbling mansion that was about to topple on him (symbolic, E F Bleiler thinks, of the decaying Anglo-Irish society at the time). His doctor, who had been treating him for heart disease, found him dead one morning. As he closed Le Fanu's staring eyes, he remarked: 'It was as I feared. The house has fallen at last.'

Sheridan Le Fanu never resolved the dilemma of being an Anglo-Irishman. On the one hand he gave his characters English names and placed them in an English countryside or in English cities; he also pursued an anti-nationalist policy in the leaders of the *Dublin University Magazine* (to which he also contributed articles, reviews, poems, stories and novels) and sent his later work to London journals. On the other hand he never lost his affection for Ireland, nor chose to live outside it. The ambivalence was apparent in his childhood and youth. His mother, an admirer of the rebels, treasured the dagger with which the patriot Lord Edward Fitzgerald had fought for his life against an English officer, yet the Le Fanus had to flee their home at Abington and remain in Dublin for three years during the Tithe Wars because of the hostility of the local people towards the ascendancy.

V S Pritchett has observed Le Fanu's Anglo-Irish versatility and his journalist's habits which made him incapable of sustaining a novel like *Uncle Silas,* which is really 'a short story that got itself into the family way'. To Pritchett Le Fanu's virtuosity is 'flawless', whereas to Elizabeth Bowen it is 'negligent'. All who have written about Le Fanu, however, concede his gifts as a writer of supernatural tales. To M R James Le Fanu is 'one of the best storytellers of the last age';

to Dorothy Sayers he is 'a master of mystery and horror'; to Nelson Browne a 'connoisseur of terror'; to Pritchett 'the Simenon of the peculiar'; to Bowen 'the greatest of them all' among the Gothics, and to Montague Summers 'a writer who stands apart from other writers of the supernatural by his ability to convey the feeling of a haunted house'.

The stories chosen for this book range over most of Le Fanu's writing career and are arranged more or less chronologically, so that you may find some of his earlier stories slightly over-mannered, as was the fashion of the time, and the later ones more spare and controlled. *The Fortunes of Sir Robert Ardagh* was his second contribution to the *Dublin University Magazine* (his first was *The Ghost and the Bonesetter*). It appeared in March 1838 and like other stories of Le Fanu's was to undergo variations and re-workings over the years: it became *The Haunted Baronet* in 1851 and later *Sir Dominic's Bargain*. It was published in the magazine as 'a second extract from the MS papers of the late Rev Francis Purcell, PP of Drumcoolagh'; Le Fanu used the fictitious Father Purcell as the narrator of all his early stories. *Ardagh* is a version of the Faust legend and shows Le Fanu's preoccupation as a young man with horror and the supernatural. I have used the abbreviated version of the story as published by Brinsley Le Fanu in 1894; it is an effective version. *Schalken the Painter* is the only story from *The Purcell Papers* not set in Ireland. It first appeared in the *Dublin University Magazine* in May 1839. It has an undercurrent of sexuality rare in Le Fanu's work with the exception of *Carmilla*. Le

Fanu, whatever his feelings, toed the Victorian line in fiction, and physical love has no place in his work. Just the same, the proportion of his stories which are set in bedrooms is astonishing.

A Ghost Story is one of the three *Ghost Stories of Chapelizod* and was first published in the *Dublin University Magazine* in January 1851 under the title *The Sexton's Adventure.* It uses as a background the village of Le Fanu's childhood, which later became the setting for *The House by the Churchyard.* When the sexton runs from the evil stranger, Le Fanu doesn't. As Forrest Reid observed, Le Fanu, when faced with horrors from which the ordinary mind recoils, 'stands tranced in terror and then moves forward with the deliberation of a sleepwalker'.

A Haunted House (its full title is *Authentic Narrative of a Haunted House*) first appeared in the *Dublin University Magazine* in October 1862 and is a report of ghostly events rather than a short story. It was published during the period in which the magazine was serialising *The House by the Churchyard. My Uncle Watson* was titled *Wicked Captain Walshawe of Wauling* when it first appeared in the same magazine in April 1864. I have given it a less risible title which I imagine will be as satisfactory as any of Le Fanu's alternative titles for his stories, titles which sometimes underwent further changes as they found their way into anthologies. In Ordean Hagen's guide to mystery fiction one of Le Fanu's longer stories is listed as having the following titles: *The Dragon Volant, The Flying Dragon, The Room at the Dragon Volant Inn* and *The Room in the Dragon Volant.* Only the last title was Le Fanu's.

The Legend of Dunblane has not been definitely authenticated as Le Fanu's, but S M Ellis, who has compiled the most comprehensive of the Le Fanu bibliographies, lists it as a possibility. It has all the characteristics of Le Fanu's work and is unusual for him only in its setting; but having set *Schalken the Painter* in Holland there was no reason why he should not have set *The Legend of Dunblane* in Scotland. It was published in *All the Year Round,* 'a weekly journal conducted by Charles Dickens' and appeared in November 1869 in the weeks following Le Fanu's *Green Tea* in the same journal, but as it seems to have been written at an earlier date and in Le Fanu's earlier style I have placed it before *Green Tea.*

Green Tea is considered by many critics to be Le Fanu's best short story; certainly it is his best psychological story. Its special qualities were noted in 1887 by Richard Dowling in an essay entitled *The Only Real Ghost in Fiction,* in which he recounted how a community of Canadian nuns had been thrown into a state of nervous misery by excessive drinking of green tea. That was after Le Fanu had written his story. As Dowling pointed out, we could all drink green tea to the end of our days and suffer nothing worse than an impaired digestion, but one of us just might be unlucky enough to conjure up some hideous familiar. Dowling considers that the ghost of the ape that slides into the clergyman's life and abides with him in *Green Tea* may be the result partly of the clergyman's excessive tea drinking, but he also recognises it as the only probable ghost in literature because it is unnecessary: it is the unconscious supernatural which has suddenly sprung into the unfortunate clergyman's life. In this story, as V S Pritchett was to observe, a 'blob of the unconscious' has floated to the surface of a man's mind. The ape is a very Freudian animal: 'dark and hairy with original sin, he skips straight out of the unchaste jungle of a pious bachelor's unconscious'.

Green Tea is narrated by a Doctor Hesselius, Father Purcell's German successor, an imaginary physician and psychologist who was invented by Sheridan Le Fanu a little too late. perhaps. With Hesselius he had truly begun to explore the dark areas of the psyche.

Madam Crowl's Ghost was originally written for *All the Year Round* in December 1870; it was incorporated in a longer story, *A Strange Adventure in the Life of Miss Laura Mildmay,* in the following year. It is told by a Mrs Jolliffe, an old north country nurse. *Dickon the Devil* was first published in the Christmas issue of *London Society* in 1872, the Christmas before Le Fanu's death a few weeks later on 7th February 1873. It was his last published story.

Sheridan Le Fanu was a careless proof-reader and occasionally guilty of inconsistencies in his work. In this book corrections have been made, some paragraphs have been shortened and the chapter headings for his story of *My Uncle Watson* have been dropped. Otherwise the stories are as they first appeared. In fact, *The Legend of Dunblane* is from a volume of *All the Year Round* which appeared to me to have been unopened since it was bound and placed in a London library in 1869. No full-length biography of Le Fanu has yet been written. We don't know if any unpublished manuscripts were discovered after his death (which took place just a few days after his last novel, uncannily titled *Willing to Die,* had been published). And if the notebook in which he kept a record of his literary transactions could be found it would make fascinating reading, for Le Fanu, as well as being a Gothic writer with visionary dreams, was also an entrepreneur.

For those interested in Le Fanu's preoccupation with the dark side of the mind, there is more than Swedenborg to study; there are the quasi-mystical writings of Jung Stillung (who married the daughter of a Huguenot family, and when she died married her friend) and his admirer, the strange Justinus Kerner, who worked as a youth in a factory attached to a madhouse and became an expert on somnambulist symptoms, demonic possession and hauntings. Kerner's *An Appearance from the Night-Realms of Nature* is an account of the intrusion of an evil and noisy spirit into a nineteenth-century German prison. Le Fanu, as we know from the *Dublin University Magazine,* had an interest in both these writers.

Le Fanu is buried not in the churchyard at Chapelizod, the scene of a novel and a number of short stories, but in Mount Jerome, a cemetery which was closer to his house in Merrion Square. His vault, for those who are fascinated by such matters, is numbered C399-122. And for those who wish to delve further into Le Fanu lore I have provided a list of sources at the end of this book.

But if you simply want to read a good ghost story, them just turn the page.

Dublin, 1975   D H

The Fortunes of Sir Robert Ardagh

The earth hath bubbles as the water hath—.
And these are of them.

IN THE SOUTH of Ireland, and on the borders of the
county of Limerick, there lies a district of two or
three miles in length, which is rendered interesting
by the fact that it is one of the very few spots
throughout this country in which some fragments of
aboriginal forests still remain. It has little or none of
the lordly character of the American forests, for the
axe has felled its oldest and its grandest trees; but in
the close wood which survives live all the wild and
pleasing peculiarities of nature: its complete
irregularity, its vistas, in whose perspective the quiet
cattle are browsing; its refreshing glades, where the
grey rocks arise from amid the nodding fern; the
silvery shafts of the old birch-trees; the knotted
trunks of the hoary oak, the grotesque but graceful
branches which never shed their honours under the
tyrant pruning-hook; the soft green sward; the
chequered light and shade; the wild luxuriant seeds;
the lichen and the moss – all are beautiful alike in the
green freshness of spring or in the sadness and sear of
autumn. Their beauty is of that kind which makes the
heart full with joy – appealing to the affections with
a power which belongs to nature only. This wood
runs up from below the base, to the ridge of a long
line of irregular hills, having perhaps, in primitive
times, formed but the skirting of some mighty forest
which occupied the level below.

But now, alas! whither have we drifted? whither
has the tide of civilization borne us? It has passed over

land unprepared for it – it has left nakedness behind it; we have lost our forests, but our marauders remain; we have destroyed all that is picturesque, while we have retained everything that is revolting in barbarism. Through the midst of this woodland there runs a deep gulley or glen, where the stillness of the scene is broken in upon by the brawling of a mountain-stream, which, however, in the winter season, swells into a rapid and formidable torrent.

There is one point at which the glen becomes extremely deep and narrow; the sides descend to the depth of some hundred feet, and are so steep as to be nearly perpendicular. The wild trees which have taken root in the crannies and chasms of the rock, have so intersected and entangled, that one can with difficulty catch a glimpse of the stream which wheels, flashes, and foams below, as if exulting in the surrounding silence and solitude.

This spot was not unwisely chosen, as a point of no ordinary strength, for the erection of a massive square tower or keep, one side of which rises as if in continuation of the precipitous cliff on which it is based. Originally, the only mode of ingress was by a narrow portal in the very wall which overtopped the precipice opening upon a ledge of rock which afforded a precarious pathway, cautiously intersected, however, by a deep trench cut out with great labour in the living rock; so that, in its pristine state, and before the introduction of artillery into the art of war, this tower might have been pronounced, and that not presumptuously, almost impregnable.

The progress of improvement, and the increasing

security of the times had, however, tempted its successive proprietors, if not to adorn, at least to enlarge their premises, and at about the middle of the last century, when the castle was last inhabited, the original square tower formed but a small part of the edifice.

The castle, and a wide tract of the surrounding country had from time immemorial, belonged to a family, which, for distinctness, was shall call by the name of Ardagh; and, owing to the associations which, in Ireland, almost always attach to scenes which have long witnessed alike, the exercise of stern feudal authority, and of that savage hospitality which distinguished the good old times, this building has become the subject and the scene of many wild and extraordinary traditions. One of them I have been enabled, by a personal acquaintance with an eye-witness of the events, to trace to its origin; and yet it is hard to say whether the events, which I am about to record, appear more strange or improbable, as seen through the distorting medium of tradition, or in the appalling dimness of uncertainty, which surrounds the reality.

Tradition says that, sometime in the last century, Sir Robert Ardagh, a young man, and the last heir of that family, went abroad and served in foreign armies; and that, having acquired considerable honour and emolument, he settled at Castle Ardagh, the building we have just now attempted to describe. He was what the country people call a *dark* man; that is, he was considered morose, reserved, and ill-tempered; and as it was supposed from the utter solitude of his life, was upon no terms of cordiality with the other members of his family.

The only occasion upon which he broke through the solitary monotony of his life, was during the continuance of the racing season, and immediately subsequent to it; at which time he was to be seen among the busiest upon the course, betting deeply and unhesitatingly, and invariably with success. Sir Robert was, however, too well-known as a man of honour, and of too high a family to be suspected of any unfair dealing. He was, moreover, a soldier, and a man of an intrepid as well as of a haughty character, and no one cared to hazard a surmise, the consequences of which would be felt most probably by its originator only.

Gossip, however, was not silent; it was remarked that Sir Robert never appeared at the race-ground, which was the only place of public resort which he frequented, except in company with a certain strange-looking person, who was never seen elsewhere, or under other circumstances. It was remarked, too, that this man, whose relation to Sir Robert was never distinctly ascertained, was the only person to whom he seemed to speak unnecessarily; it was observed that while with the country gentry he exchanged no further communication than what was unavoidable in arranging his sporting transactions, with this person he would converse earnestly and frequently.

Tradition asserts that, to enhance the curiosity which this unaccountable and exclusive preference excited, the stranger possessed some striking and unpleasant peculiarities of person and of garb – she does not say, however, what these were – but they, in conjunction with Sir Robert's secluded habits, and extraordinary run of luck – a success which was supposed to result from the suggestions and immediate advice of the unknown – were sufficient to warrant report in pronouncing that there was something *queer* in the wind, and in surmising that Sir Robert was playing a fearful and a hazardous game, and that, in short, his strange companion was little better than the Devil himself.

Years, however, rolled quietly away, and nothing novel occurred in the arrangements of Castle Ardagh, excepting that Sir Robert parted with his odd companion, but as nobody could tell whence he came, so nobody could say whither he had gone. Sir Robert's habits, however, underwent no consequent change; he continued regularly to frequent the race meetings, without mixing at all in the convivialities of the gentry, and immediately afterwards to relapse into the secluded monotony of his ordinary life.

It was said that he had accumulated vast sums of money – and, as his bets were always successful and always large, such must have been the case. He did not suffer the acquisition of wealth, however, to influence his hospitality or his housekeeping – he neither purchased land, nor extended his establishment; and his mode of enjoying his money must have been altogether that of the miser – consisting, merely, in the pleasure of touching and telling his gold, and in the consciousness of wealth.

Sir Robert's temper, so far from improving, became

'. . . in its fingers was clutched . . . a long lock of coarse sooty hair . . .'

(see p. 36)

more than ever gloomy and morose. He sometimes carried the indulgence of his evil dispositions to such a height that it bordered upon insanity. During these paroxysms, he would neither eat, drink, nor sleep. On such occasions he insisted on perfect privacy, even from the intrusion of his most trusted servants; his voice was frequently heard, sometimes in earnest supplication, sometimes raised, as if in loud and angry altercation, with some unknown visitant. Sometimes he would for hours together walk to and fro throughout the long oak-wainscoted apartment, which he generally occupied, with wild gesticulations and agitated pace, in the manner of one who has been roused to a state of unnatural excitement, by some sudden and appalling intimation.

These paroxysms of apparent lunacy were so frightful, that during their continuance even his oldest and most faithful domestics dared not approach him; consequently his hours of agony were never intruded upon, and the mysterious causes of his suffering appeared likely to remain hidden for ever.

On one occasion a fit of this kind continued for an unusual time; the ordinary term of their duration – about two days – had been long past, and the old servant who generally waited upon Sir Robert after these visitations, having in vain listened for the well-known tinkle of his master's hand-bell, began to feel extremely anxious; he feared that his master might have died from sheer exhaustion, or perhaps put an end to his own existence during his miserable depression. These fears at length became so strong, that having in vain urged some of his brother-servants to accompany him, he determined to go up alone, and himself see whether any accident had befallen Sir Robert.

He traversed the several passages which conducted from the new to the more ancient parts of the mansion; and having arrived in the old hall of the castle, the utter silence of the hour – for it was very late in the night – the idea of the nature of the enterprise in which he was engaging himself, a sensation of remoteness from anything like human companionship, but, more than all, the vivid but undefined anticipation of something horrible, came upon him with such oppressive weight that he hesitated as to whether he should proceed.

Real uneasiness, however, respecting the fate of his master, for whom he felt that kind of attachment, which the force of habitual intercourse not unfrequently engenders respecting objects not in themselves amiable, and also a latent unwillingness to expose his weakness to the ridicule of his fellow-servants, combined to overcome his reluctance; and he had just placed his foot upon the first step of the staircase which conducted to his master's chamber, when his attention was arrested by a low but distinct knocking at the hall-door. Not, perhaps, very sorry at finding thus an excuse even for deferring his intended expedition, he placed the candle upon a stone block which lay in the hall and approached the door, uncertain whether his ears had not deceived him. This doubt was justified by the circumstance, that the hall entrance had been for nearly fifty years disused as a mode of ingress to the castle. The situation of this

31

gate also, which we have endeavoured to describe, opening upon a narrow ledge of rock which overhangs a perilous cliff, rendered it at all times, but particularly at night, a dangerous entrance. This shelving platform of rock, which formed the only avenue to the door, was divided, as I have already stated, by a broad chasm, the planks across which had long disappeared, by decay or otherwise, so that it seemed at least highly improbable that any man could have found his way across the passage in safety to the door – more particularly on a night like that, of singular darkness.

The old man, therefore, listened attentively; to ascertain whether the first application should be followed by another. He had not long to wait. The same low but singularly distinct knocking was repeated; so low that it seemed as if the applicant had employed no harder or heavier instrument than his hand, and yet, despite the immense thickness of the door, with such strength that the sound was distinctly audible. The knock was repeated a third time, without any increase of loudness; and the old man, obeying an impulse for which to his dying hour he could never account, proceeded to remove, one by one, the three great oaken bars which secured the door. Time and damp had effectually corroded the iron chambers of the lock, so that it afforded little resistance. With some effort, as he believed, assisted from without, the old servant succeeded in opening the door; and a low, square-built figure, apparently that of a man wrapped in a large black cloak, entered the hall.

The servant could not see much of this visitant with any distinctness; his dress appeared foreign, the skirt of his ample cloak was thrown over one shoulder; he wore a large felt hat, with a very heavy leaf, from under which escaped what appeared to be a mass of long sooty-black hair; his feet were cased in heavy riding-boots. Such were the few particulars which the servant had time and light to observe. The stranger desired him to let his master know instantly that a friend has come, by appointment, to settle some business with him. The servant hesitated, but a slight motion on the part of his visitor, as if to possess himself of the candle, determined him; so taking it in his hand, he ascended the castle stairs, leaving his guest in the hall.

On reaching the apartment which opened upon the oak-chamber he was surprised to observe the door of that room partly open, and the room itself lit up. He paused, but there was no sound; he looked in, and saw Sir Robert, his head, and the upper part of his body reclining on a table, upon which two candles burned; his arms were stretched forward on either side, and perfectly motionless; it appeared that having been sitting at the table, he had thus sunk forward, either dead or in a swoon. There was no sound of breathing; all was silent, except the sharp ticking of a watch, which lay beside the lamp. The servant coughed twice or thrice, but with no effect; his fears now almost amounted to certainty, and he was approaching the table on which his master partly lay, to satisfy himself of his death, when Sir Robert slowly raised his head, and throwing himself back in his chair, fixed his eyes in a ghastly and uncertain gaze upon his attendant. At length he said, slowly and painfully, as if he dreaded the answer:

'In God's name, what are you?'

'Sir,' said the servant, 'a strange gentleman wants to see you below.'

At this intimation, Sir Robert, starting on his feet and tossing his arms wildly upwards, uttered a shriek of such appalling and despairing terror that it was almost too fearful for human endurance; and long after the sound had ceased, it seemed to the terrified imagination of the old servant to roll through the deserted passages in bursts of unnatural laughter. After a few moments, Sir Robert said:

'Can't you send him away? Why does he come so soon? O God! O God! let him leave me for an hour; a little time. I can't see him now; try to get him away. You see I can't go down now; I have not strength. O God! O God! let him come back in an hour; it is not long to wait. He cannot lose anything by it; nothing, nothing, nothing. Tell him that! Say anything to him.'

The servant went down. In his own words, he did not feel the stairs under him till he got to the hall. The figure stood exactly as he had left it. He delivered his master's message as coherently as he could. The stranger replied in a careless tone:

'If Sir Robert will not come down to me, I must go up to him.'

The man returned, and to his surprise he found his master much more composed in manner. He listened to the message, and though the cold perspiration rose in drops upon his forehead faster than he could wipe it away, his manner had lost the dreadful agitation which had marked it before. He rose feebly, and casting a last look of agony behind him, passed from the room to the lobby, where he signed to his attendant not to follow him. The man moved as far as the head of the staircase, from whence he had a tolerably distinct view of the hall, which was imperfectly lighted by the candle he had left there.

He saw his master reel, rather than walk, down the stairs, clinging all the way to the banisters. He walked on, as if about to sink every moment from weakness. The figure advanced as if to meet him, and in passing struck down the light. The servant could see no more; but there was a sound of struggling, renewed at intervals with silent but fearful energy. It was evident, however, that the parties were approaching the door, for he heard the solid oak sound twice or thrice, as the feet of the combatants, in shuffling hither and thither over the floor, struck upon it. After a slight pause he heard the door thrown open with such violence that the leaf seemed to strike the side-wall of the hall, for it was so dark without that this could only be surmised by the sound. The struggle was renewed with an agony and intenseness of energy that betrayed itself in deep-drawn gasps. One desperate effort, which terminated in the breaking of some part of the door, producing a sound as if the door-post was wrenched from its position, was followed by another wrestle, evidently upon the narrow ledge which ran outside the door, overtopping the precipice. This proved to be the final struggle, for it was followed by a crashing sound as if some heavy body had fallen over, and was rushing down the precipice through the light boughs that crossed near the top. All then became still as the grave, except when the moan of the night wind sighed up the wooded glen.

The old servant had not the nerve to return through the hall, and to him that night seemed all but endless; but morning at length came, and with it the disclosure of the events of the night. Near the door, upon the ground, lay Sir Robert's sword-belt, which had given way in the scuffle. A huge splinter from the massive door-post had been wrenched off, by an almost superhuman effort – one which nothing but the gripe of a despairing man could have severed – and on the rock outside were left the marks of the slipping and sliding of feet.

At the foot of the precipice, not immediately under the castle, but dragged some way up the glen, were found the remains of Sir Robert, with hardly a vestige of a limb or feature left distinguishable. The right hand, however, was uninjured, and in its fingers was clutched, with the fixedness of death, a long lock of coarse sooty hair – the only direct circumstantial evidence of the presence of a second person.

2
Schalken
the Painter

YOU WILL NO doubt be surprised, my dear friend, at the subject of the following narrative. What had I to do with Schalken, or Schalken with me? He had returned to his native land, and was probably dead and buried before I was born; I never visited Holland, nor spoke with a native of that country. So much I believe you already know. I must, then, give you my authority, and state to you frankly the ground upon which rests the credibility of the strange story which I am about to lay before you.

I was acquainted, in my early days, with a Captain Vandael, whose father had served King William in the Low Countries, and also in my unhappy land during the Irish campaigns. I know not how it happened that I liked this man's society, in spite of his politics and religion: but so it was; and it was by means of the free intercourse to which our intimacy gave rise that I became possessed of the curious tale which you are about to hear.

I had often been struck, while visiting Vandael, by a remarkable picture, in which, though no connoisseur myself, I could not fail to discern some very strong pecularities, particularly in the distribution of light and shade, as also a certain oddity in the design itself, which interested my curiosity. It represented the interior of what might be a chamber in some antique religious building – the foreground was occupied by a female figure, arrayed in a species of white robe, part of which was arrayed so as to form a veil. The dress, however, is not strictly that of any religious order. In its hand the figure bears a lamp, by whose light alone the form and face are illuminated;

the features are marked by an arch smile, such as pretty women wear when engaged in successfully practising some roguish trick; in the background, and, excepting where the dim light of an expiring fire serves to define the form, totally in the shade, stands the figure of a man equipped in the old fashion, with doublet and so forth, in the attitude of alarm, his hand being placed upon the hilt of his sword, which he appears to be in the act of drawing.

'There are some pictures,' said I to my friend, 'which impress one, I know not how, with a conviction that they represent not the mere ideal shapes and combinations which have floated through the imagination of the artist, but scenes, faces, and situations, which have actually existed. When I look upon that picture, something assures me that I behold the representation of a reality.'

Vandael smiled, and, fixing his eyes upon the painting musingly, he said:

'Your fancy has not deceived you, my good friend, for that picture is the record, and I believe a faithful one, of a remarkable and mysterious occurrence. It was painted by Schalken, and contains, in the face of the female figure which occupies the most prominent place in the design, an accurate portrait of Rose Velderkaust, the niece of Gerard Douw, the first and, I believe, the only love of Godfrey Schalken. My father knew the painter well, and from Schalken himself he learned the story of the mysterious drama, one scene of which the picture has embodied. This painting, which is accounted a fine specimen of Schalken's style, was bequeathed to my father by the

artist's will, and, as you have observed, is a very
striking and interesting production.'

I had only to request Vandael to tell the story of
the painting in order to be gratified; and thus it is
that I am enabled to submit to you a faithful recital
of what I heard myself, leaving you to reject or to
allow the evidence upon which the truth of the
tradition depends, with this one assurance, that
Schalken was an honest, blunt Dutchman, and, I
believe, wholly incapable of committing a flight of
imagination; and further, that Vandael, from whom I
heard the story, appeared firmly convinced of its
truth.

There are few forms upon which the mantle of
mystery and romance could seem to hang more
ungracefully than upon that of the uncouth and
clownish Schalken – the Dutch boor – the rude and
dogged, but most cunning worker in oils, whose
pieces delight the initiated of the present day almost
as much as his manners disgusted the refined of his
own; and yet this man, so rude, so dogged, so
slovenly, I had almost said so savage, in mien and
manner, during his after successes, had been selected
by the capricious goddess in his early life, to figure as
the hero of a romance by no means devoid of interest
or of mystery.

Who can tell how meet he may have been in his
young days to play the part of the lover or the hero
– who can say that in early life he had been the same
harsh, unlicked, and rugged boor that, in his maturer
age, he proved – or how far the neglected rudeness
which afterwards marked his air, and garb, and

manners, may not have been the growth of that reckless apathy not infrequently produced by bitter misfortunes and disappointments in early life?

These questions can never be answered.

We must content ourselves, then, with a plain statement of facts, leaving matters of speculation to those who like them.

When Schalken studied under the immortal Gerard Douw, he was a young man; and, in spite of the phlegmatic constitution and excitable manner which he shared, we believe, with his countrymen, he was not incapable of deep and vivid impressions, for it is an established fact that the young painter looked with considerable interest upon the beautiful niece of his wealthy master.

Rose Velderkaust was very young, having, at the period of which we speak, not yet attained her seventeenth year; and, if tradition speaks truth, she possessed all the soft dimpling charms of the fair, light-haired Flemish maidens. Schalken had not studied long in the school of Gerard Douw when he felt this interest deepening into something of a keener and intenser feeling that was quite consistent with that tranquillity of his honest Dutch heart; and at the same time he perceived, or thought he perceived, flattering symptoms of a reciprocity of liking, and this was quite sufficient to determine whatever indecision he might have heretofore experienced, and to lead him to devote exclusively to every hope and feeling of his heart. In short, he was as much in love as a Dutchman could be. He was not long in making his passion known to the pretty maiden herself, and his declaration was followed by a corresponding confession upon her part.

Schalken, however, was a poor man, and he possessed no counterbalancing advantage of birth or position to induce the old man to consent to a union which must involve his niece and ward in the strugglings and difficulties of a young and nearly friendless artist. He was, therefore, to wait until time had furnished him with the opportunity, and accident with success; and then, if his labours were found sufficiently lucrative, it was to be hoped that his proposals might at least be listened to by her jealous guardian. Months passed away, and, cheered by the smiles of the little Rose, Schalken's labours were redoubled, and with such effect and improvement as reasonably to promise the realisation of his hopes, and no contemptible eminence in his art, before many years should have elapsed.

The even course of this cheering prosperity was, unfortunately, designed to experience a sudden and formidable interruption and that, too, in a manner so strange and mysterious, as to baffle all investigation, and throw upon the events themselves a shadow of almost supernatural horror.

Shalken had one evening remained in the master's studio considerably longer than his more volatile companions, who had gladly availed themselves of the excuse which the dusk of evening afforded to withdraw from their several tasks, in order to finish a day of labour in the jollity and conviviality of the tavern.

But Schalken worked for improvement, or rather

for love. Besides, he was now engaged merely in sketching a design, an operation which, unlike that of colouring, might be continued as long as there was light sufficient to distinguish between canvas and charcoal. He had not then, nor, indeed, until long after, discovered the peculiar powers of his pencil; and he was engaged in composing a group of extremely roguish-looking and grotesque imps and demons, who were inflicting various ingenious torments upon a perspiring and pot-bellied St. Anthony, who reclined in the midst of them, apparently in the last stage of drunkenness.

The young artist, however, though incapable of executing, or even of appreciating, anything of true sublimity, had nevertheless discernment enough to prevent his being by any means satisfied with his work; and many were the patient erasures and corrections which the limbs and features of saint and devil underwent, yet all without producing in their arrangement anything of improvement or increased effect.

The large, old-fashioned room was silent, and, with the exception of himself, quite deserted by its usual inmates. An hour had passed – nearly two – without any improved result. Daylight had already declined, and twilight was fast giving away to the darkness of night. The patience of the young man was exhausted, and he stood before his unfinished production, absorbed in no very pleasing ruminations, one hand buried in the folds of his long dark hair, and the other holding the piece of charcoal which had so ill executed his office, and which he now rubbed without much regard to the sable streaks which it produced, with irritable pressure upon his ample Flemish inexpressibles.

'Pshaw!' said the young man aloud, 'would that picture, devils, saints, and all, were where they should be – in hell!'

A short, sudden laugh, uttered startlingly close to his ear, instantly responded to the ejaculation.

The artist turned sharply round, and now for the first time became aware that his labours had been overlooked by a stranger.

Within about a yard and a half, and rather behind him, there stood what was, or appeared to be, the figure of an elderly man: he wore a short cloak, and broad-brimmed hat with a conical crown, and in his hand, which was protected by a heavy, gauntlet-shaped glove, he carried a long ebony walking-stick, surmounted by what appeared, as it glittered dimly in the twilight, to be a massive head of gold; and upon his breast, through the folds of the cloak, there shone the links of a rich chain of the same metal.

The room was so obscure that nothing further of the appearance of the figure could be ascertained, and the face was altogether overshadowed by the heavy flap of the beaver which overhung it, so that no feature could be clearly discerned. A quantity of dark hair escaped from beneath this sombre hat, a circumstance which, connected with the firm, upright carriage of the intruder, proved that his years could not yet exceed threescore or thereabouts.

There was an air of gravity and importance about the garb of this person, and something indescribably

44

odd – I might say awful – in the perfect, stone-like movelessness of the figure, that effectively checked the testy comment which had at once risen to the lips of the irritated artist. He therefore, as soon as he had sufficiently recovered from his surprise, asked the stranger, civilly, to be seated, and desired to know if he had any message to leave for his master.

'Tell Gerard Douw,' said the unknown, without altering his attitude in the smallest degree, 'that Mynher Vanderhausen, of Rotterdam, desires to speak with him to-morrow evening at this hour, and if he please, in this room, upon matters of weight; that is all. Good-night.'

The stranger, having finished this message, turned abruptly, and, with a quick but silent step quitted the room before Schalken had time to say a word in reply.

The young man felt a curiosity to see in what direction the burgher of Rotterdam would turn on quitting the studio, and for that purpose he went directly to the window which commanded the door.

A lobby of considerable extent intervened between the inner door of the painter's room and the street entrance, so that Schalken occupied the post of observation before the old man could possibly have reached the street.

He watched in vain, however. There was no other mode of exit.

Had the old man vanished, or was he lurking about the recesses of the lobby for some bad purpose? This last suggestion filled the mind of Schalken with a vague horror, which was so unaccountably intense as to make him alike afraid to remain in the room alone and reluctant to pass through the lobby.

However, with an effort which appeared very disproportioned to the occasion, he summoned resolution to leave the room, and, having double-locked the door, and thrust the key in his pocket, without looking to the right or left, he traversed the passage which had so recently, perhaps still, contained the person of his mysterious visitant, scarcely venturing to breathe till he had arrived in the open street.

'Mynher Vanderhausen,' said Gerard Douw, within himself, as the appointed hour approached; 'Mynher Vanderhausen, of Rotterdam! I never heard of the man till yesterday. What can he want of me? A portrait, perhaps, to be painted; or a younger son or a poor relation to be apprenticed; or a collection to be valued; or-pshaw! there's no one in Rotterdam to leave me a legacy. Well, whatever the business may be, we shall soon know it all.'

It was now the close of day, and every easel except that of Schalken was deserted. Gerard Douw was pacing the apartment with the restless step of impatient expectation, every now and then humming a passage from a piece of music which he was himself composing for, though no great proficient, he admired the art – sometimes pausing to glance over the work of one of his absent pupils, but more frequently placing himself at the window, from whence he might observe the passengers who threaded the obscure street in which his studio was placed.

'Said you not, Godfrey,' exclaimed Douw, after a

long and fruitless gaze from his post of observation, and turning to Schalken – 'said you not the hour of appointment was about seven by the clock of the Stadhouse?'

'It had just told seven when I first saw him, sir,' answered the student.

'The hour is close at hand, then,' said the master, consulting a horolage as large and as round as a full-grown orange. 'Mynher Vanderhausen from Rotterdam – is it not so?'

'Such was the name.'

'And an elderly man, richly clad?' continued Douw.

'As well as I might see,' replied his pupil. 'He could not be young, nor yet very old neither, and his dress was rich and grave, as might become a citizen of wealth and consideration.'

At this moment the sonorous boom of the Stadhouse clock told, stroke after stroke, the hour of seven; the eyes of both master and student were directed to the door; and it was not until the last peal of the bell had ceased to vibrate that Douw exclaimed:

'So, so; we shall have his worship presently – that is, if he means to keep his hour; if not, thou mayst wait for him, Godfrey, if you court the acquaintance of a capricious burgomaster. As for me, I think our old Leyden contains a sufficiency of such commodities without an importation from Rotterdam.'

Schalken laughed, as if in duty bound; and, after a pause of some minutes, Douw suddenly exclaimed:

'What if it should all prove a jest, a piece of mummery got up by Vankarp, or some such worthy! I wish you had run all risks and cudgeled the old burgomaster, stadholder, or whatever else he may be, soundly. I would wager a dozen of Rhenish, his worship would have pleaded old acquaintance before the third application.'

'Here he comes, sir' said Schalken, in a low, admonitory tone; and instantly, upon turning towards the door, Gerard Douw observed the same figure which had, on the day before, so unexpectedly greeted the vision of his pupil Schalken.

There was something in the air and mien of the figure which at once satisfied the painter that there was no mummery in the case, and that he really stood in the presence of a man of worship; and so, without hesitation, he doffed his cap, and courteously saluting the stranger, requested him to be seated.

The visitor waved his hand slightly, as if in acknowledgment of the courtesy, but remained standing.

'I have the honour to see Mynher Vanderhausen, of Rotterdam?' said Gerard Douw.

'The same,' was the laconic reply.

'I understand your worship desires to speak with me,' continued Douw, 'and I am here by appointment to wait your commands.'

'Is that a man of trust?' said Vanderhausen, turning towards Schalken, who stood at a little distance behind his master.

'Certainly,' replied Gerard.

'Then let him take this box and get the nearest jeweller or goldsmith to value its contents, and let him return hither with a certificate of the valuation.'

At the same time he placed a small case, about nine inches square, in the hands of Gerard Douw, who was as much amazed at its weight as at the strange abruptness with which it was handed to him.

In accordance with the wishes of the stranger, he delivered it into the hands of Schalken, and repeating his directions, despatched him upon the mission.

Schalken disposed his precious charge securely beneath the folds of his cloak, and rapidly traversing two or three narrow streets, he stopped at a corner house, the lower part of which was then occupied by the shop of a Jewish goldsmith.

Schalken entered the shop and calling the little Hebrew into the obscurity of its back recesses, he proceeded to lay before him Vanderhausen's packet.

On being examined by the light of a lamp, it appeared entirely encased with lead, the outer surface of which was much scraped and soiled, and nearly white with age. This was with difficulty partially removed, and disclosed beneath a box of some dark and singularly hard wood; this, too, was forced, and after the removal of two or three folds of linen, its contents proved to be a mass of golden ingots, close packed, and, as the Jew declared, of the most perfect quality.

Every ingot underwent the scrutiny of the little Jew, who seemed to feel an epicurean delight in touching and testing these morsels of the glorious metal, and each one of them was replaced in the box with the exclamation:

'Mein Gott, how very perfect! not one grain of alloy – beautiful, beautiful!'

The task was at length finished, and the Jew certified under his hand the value of the ingots submitted to his examination to amount to many thousand rix-dollars.

With the desired document in his bosom, and the rich box of gold carefully pressed under his arm, and concealed by his cloak, he retraced his way, and entering the studio, found his master and the stranger in close conference.

Schalken had no sooner left the room, in order to execute the commission he had taken in charge than Vanderhausen addressed Gerard Douw in the following terms:

'I may not tarry with you to-night more than a few minutes, and so I shall briefly tell you the matter upon which I come. You visited the town of Rotterdam some four months ago, and then I saw in the church of St Lawrence your niece, Rose Velderkaust. I desire to marry her, and if I satisfy you as to the fact that I am very wealthy – more wealthy than any husband you could dream of for her – I expect that you will forward my views to the utmost of your authority. If you approve my proposal, you must close with it at once, for I cannot command time enough to wait for calculations and delays.'

Gerard Douw was, perhaps, as much astonished as anyone could be by the very unexpected nature of Mynher Vanderhausen's communication; but he did not give vent to any unseemly expression of surprise, for, besides the motives supplied by prudence and politeness, the painter experienced a kind of chill and oppressive sensation, something like that which is supposed to affect a man who is placed unconsciously in immediate contact with something to which he has a natural antipathy – an undefined horror and dread

50

while standing in the presence of the eccentric stranger, which made him very unwilling to say anything which might reasonably prove offensive.

'I have no doubt,' said Gerard, after two or three prefatory hems, 'that the connection which you propose would prove alike advantageous and honourable to my niece; but you must be aware that she has a will of her own, and may not acquiese in what *we* may design for her advantage.'

'Do not seek to deceive me, Sir Painter,' said Vanderhausen; 'you are her guardian – she is your ward. She is mine if *you* like to make her so.'

The man of Rotterdam moved forward a little as he spoke, and Gerard Douw, he scarce knew why, inwardly prayed for the speedy return of Schalken.

'I desire,' said the mysterious gentleman, 'to place in your hands at once an evidence of my wealth, and a security for my liberal dealings with your niece. The lad will return in a minute or two with a sum in value five times the fortune which she has a right to expect from a husband. This shall be in your hands, together with her dowry, and you may apply the united sum as suits her interest best; it shall be all exclusively hers while she lives. Is that liberal?'

Douw assented, and inwardly thought that fortune had been extraordinarily kind to his niece. The stranger, he thought, must be both wealthy and generous, and such an offer was not to be despised, though made by a humorist, and one of no very prepossessing presence.

Rose had no very high pretensions, for she was almost without dowry; indeed, altogether so, excepting so far as the deficiency had been supplied by the generosity of her uncle. Neither had she any right to raise any scruples against the match on the score of birth, for her own origin was by no means elevated, and as to other objections, Gerard resolved, and, indeed, by the usages of the time was warranted in resolving, not to listen to them for a moment.

'Sir,' said he, addressing the stranger, 'your offer is most liberal, and whatever hesitation I may feel in closing with it immediately, arises solely from not having the honour of knowing anything of your family or station. Upon these points you can, of course, satisfy me without difficulty?'

'As to my respectability,' said the stranger, drily, 'you must take that for granted at present, pester me with no inquiries; you can discover nothing more about me than I choose to make known. You shall have sufficient security for my respectability – my word, if you are honourable; if you are sordid, my gold.'

'A testy old gentleman,' thought Douw; 'he must have his own way. But, all things considered, I am justified in giving my niece to him. Were she my own daughter, I would do the like by her. I will not pledge myself unnecessarily, however.'

'You will not pledge yourself unnecessarily,' said Vanderhausen, strangely uttering the very words which had just floated through the mind of his companion, 'but you will do so if it *is* necessary, I presume; and I will show you that I consider it indispensable. If the gold I mean to leave in your hands satisfy you, and if you desire that my proposal shall not be at once withdrawn, you must, before I leave this room, write your name to this engagement.'

Having thus spoken, he placed a paper in the hands of Gerard, the contents of which expressed an engagement entered into by Gerard Douw, to give to Wilken Vanderhausen, of Rotterdam, in marriage Rose Velderkaust, and so forth, within one week of the date hereof.

While the painter was employed in reading this covenant, Schalken, as we have stated, entered the studio, and having delivered the box and the valuation of the Jew into the hands of the stranger, he was about to retire, when Vanderhausen called to him to wait; and presenting the case and the certificate to Gerard Douw, he waited in silence until he had satisfied himself by an inspection of both as to the value of the pledge left in his hands. At length he said:

'Are you content?'

The painter said he would fain have another day to consider.

'Not an hour,' said the suitor, coolly.

'Well, then,' said Douw, 'I am content; it is a bargain.'

'Then sign at once,' said Vanderhausen; 'I am weary.'

At the same time he produced a small case of writing materials, and Gerard signed the important document.

'Let this youth witness the covenant,' said the old man; and Godfrey Schalken unconsciously signed the instrument which bestowed upon another that hand which he had so long regarded as the object and reward of all his labours.

The compact being thus completed, the strange visitor folded up the paper, and stowed it safely in an inner pocket.

'I will visit you tomorrow night, at nine of the clock, at your house, Gerard Douw, and you will see the subject of our contract. Farewell.' And so saying, Wilken Vanderhausen moved stiffly, but rapidly, out of the room.

Schalken, eager to resolve his doubts, had placed himself by the window in order to watch the street entrance; but the experiment served only to support his suspicions, for the old man did not issue from the door. This was very strange, very odd, very fearful. He and his master returned together, and talked but little on the way, for each had his own subjects of reflection, of anxiety, and of hope.

Schalken, however, did not know the ruin which threatened his cherished schemes.

Gerard Douw knew nothing of the attachment which had sprung up between his pupil and his niece; and even if he had, it is doubtful whether he would have regarded its existence as any serious obstruction to the wishes of Mynher Vanderhausen.

Marriages were then and there matters of traffic and calculation; and it would have appeared as absurd in the eye of the guardian to make a mutual attachment an essential element in a contract of marriage, as it would have been to draw up his bond and receipts in the language of chivalrous romance.

The painter, however, did not communicate to his niece the important step which he had taken on her

'...She disclosed...sitting bolt upright in bed, the livid and demoniac form of Vanderhausen...'

(see p. 72)

behalf, and his resolution arose not from any anticipation of opposition on her part, but solely from a ludicrous consciousness that if his ward were, as she very naturally might do, to ask him to describe the appearance of the bridegroom whom he destined for her, he would be forced to confess that he had not seen his face, and, if called upon, would find it impossible to indentify him.

Upon the next day, Gerard Douw having dined, called his niece to him, and having scanned her person with an air of satisfaction, he took her hand, and looking upon her pretty, innocent face with a smile of kindness, he said:

'Rose, my girl, that face of yours will make your fortune.' Rose blushed and smiled. 'Such faces and such tempers seldom go together, and, when they do, the compound is a love potion which few heads or hearts can resist. Trust me, thou will soon be a bride, girl. But this is trifling, and I am pressed for time, so make ready the large room by eight o'clock to-night, and give directions for supper at nine. I expect a friend to-night; and, observe me, child, do thou trick thyself out handsomely. I would not have him think us poor or sluttish.'

With these words he left the chamber and took his way to the room to which we have already had occasion to introduce our readers – that in which his pupils worked.

When evening closed in, Gerard called Schalken, who was about to take his departure to his obscure and comfortless lodgings, and asked him to come home and sup with Rose and Vanderhausen.

The invitation was of course accepted and Gerard Douw and his pupil soon found themselves in the handsome and somewhat antique-looking room which had been prepared for the reception of the stranger.

A cheerful wood-fire blazed in the capacious hearth; a little at one side an old-fashioned table, with richly-carved legs was placed – destined, no doubt, to receive the supper, for which preparations were going forward; and ranged with exact regularity, stood the tall-backed chairs, whose ungracefulness was more than counterbalanced by their comfort.

The little party, consisting of Rose, her uncle, and the artist, awaited the arrival of the expected visitor with considerable impatience.

Nine o'clock at length came, and with it a summons at the street door, which, being speedily answered, was followed by a slow and emphatic tread upon the staircase; the steps moved heavily across the lobby, the door of the room in which the party which we have described were assembled slowly opened, and there entered a figure which startled, almost appalled, the phlegmatic Dutchmen, and nearly made Rose scream with affright; it was the form, and arrayed in the garb, of Mynher Vanderhausen; the air, the gait, the height was the same, but the features had never been seen by any of the party before.

The stranger stopped at the door of the room, and displayed his form and face completely. He wore a dark-coloured cloth cloak, which was short and full, not falling quite to his knees; his legs were cased in dark purple silk stockings, and his shoes were adorned with roses of the same colour. The opening of the cloak in front showed the under-suit to consist of some very dark, perhaps sable material, and his hands were enclosed in a pair of heavy leather gloves which ran up considerably above the wrist, in the manner of a gauntlet. In one hand he carried his walking stick and his hat, which he had removed, and the other hung heavily by his side. A quantity of grizzled hair descended in long tresses from his head, and its folds rested upon the plaits of a stiff ruff, which effectually concealed his neck.

So far all was well; but the face! – all the flesh of the face was coloured with the bluish leaden hue which is sometimes produced by the operation of metallic medicines administered in excessive quantities; the eyes were enormous, and the white appeared both above and below the iris, which gave to them an expression of insanity, which was heightened by the glassy fixedness; the nose was well enough, but the mouth was writhed considerably to one side, where it opened in order to give egress to two long, discoloured fangs, which projected from the upper jaw, far below the lower lip; the hue of the lips themselves bore the usual relation to that of the face, and was consequently nearly black. The character of the face was malignant, even satanic to the last degree; and indeed, such a combination of horror could hardly be accounted for, except by supposing the corpse of some atrocious malefactor, which had long hung blackening upon the gibbet, to have at length become the habitation of a demon – the frightful sport of satanic possession.

It was remarkable that the worshipful stranger suffered as little as possible of his flesh to appear, and that during his visit he did not once remove his gloves.

Having stood for some moments at the door, Gerard Douw at length found breath and collectedness to bid him welcome and, with a mute inclination of the head, the stranger stepped forward into the room.

There was something indescribably odd, even horrible, about all his motions, something undefinable, that was unnatural, unhuman – it was as if the limbs were guided and directed by a spirit unused to the management of bodily machinery.

The stranger hardly said anything during his visit, which did not exceed half an hour; and the host himself could scarcely muster courage enough to utter the few necessary salutations and courtesies; and, indeed, such was the nervous tension which the presence of Vanderhausen inspired, that very little would have made all his entertainers fly bellowing from the room.

They had not so far lost all self-possession, however, as to fail to observe two strange peculiarities of their visitor.

During his stay he did not once suffer his eye-lids to close, nor even to move in the slightest degree; and further, there was a death-like stillness in his whole person, owing to the total absence of the heaving motion of the chest, caused by the process of respiration.

These two peculiarities, though when told they

may appear trifling, produced a very striking and unpleasant effect when seen and observed. Vanderhausen at length relieved the painter of Leyden of his inauspicious presence; and with no small gratification the little party heard the street-door close after him.

'Dear uncle,' said Rose, 'what a frightful man! I would not see him again for the wealth of the States!'

'Tush, foolish girl!' said Douw, whose sensations were anything but comfortable. 'A man may be as ugly as the devil, and yet if his heart and actions are good, he is worth all the pretty-faced, perfumed puppies that walk the Mall. Rose, my girl, it is very true he has not thy pretty face, but I know him to be wealthy and liberal; and were he ten times more ugly—'

'Which is inconceivable,' observed Rose.

'These two virtues would be sufficient,' continued her uncle, 'to counterbalance all his deformity; and if not of power sufficient actually to alter the shape of his features, at least of efficacy enough to prevent one thinking them amiss.'

'Do you know, uncle,' said Rose, 'when I saw him standing at the door, I could not get out of my head that I saw the old, painted, wooden figure that used to frighten me so much in the church af St Laurence of Rotterdam.'

Gerard laughed, though he could not help inwardly acknowledging the justness of the comparison. He was resolved, however, as far as he could, to check his niece's inclination to ridicule the ugliness of her intended bridegroom, although he was not a little pleased to observe that she appeared totally exempt from that mysterious dread of the stranger which, he could not disguise it from himself, considerably affected him as also his pupil Godfrey Schalken.

Early on the next day there arrived, from various quarters of the town, rich presents of silks, velvets, jewellery, and so forth, for Rose; and also a packet directed to Gerard Douw, which, on being opened, was found to contain a contract of marriage, formally drawn up, between Wilken Vanderhausen of the Boom-quay, in Rotterdam, and Rose Velderkaust of Leyden, niece to Gerard Douw, master in the art of painting, also of the same city; and containing engagements on the part of Vanderhausen to make settlements upon his bride, for more splendour than he had before led her guardian to believe likely, and which were to be secured to her use in the most exceptional manner possible – the money being placed in the hands of Gerard Douw himself.

I have no sentimental scenes to describe, no cruelty of guardians, or magnanimity of wards, or agonies of lovers. The record I have to make is one of sordidness, levity and interest. In less than a week after the first interview which we have just described the contract of marriage was fulfilled and Schalken saw the prize which he would have risked anything to secure, carried off triumphantly by his formidable rival.

For two or three days he absented himself from the school; he then returned and worked, if with less cheerfulness, with far more dogged determination

61

than before; the dream of love had given place to that of ambition.

Months passed away and, contrary to his expectations, and, indeed, to the direct promise of the parties, Gerard Douw heard nothing of his niece, or her worshipful spouse. The interest of the money, which was to have been demanded in quarterly sums, lay unclaimed in his hands. He began to grow extremely uneasy.

Mynher Vanderhausen's direction in Rotterdam he was fully possessed of. After some irresolution he finally determined to journey thither – a trifling undertaking and easily accomplished – and thus to satisfy himself of the safety and comfort of his ward, for whom he entertained an honest and strong affection.

His search was in vain, however. No one in Rotterdam had ever heard of Mynher Vanderhausen.

Gerard Douw left not a house on the Boom-quay untried; but all in vain. No one could give him any confirmation whatever touching the object of his inquiry, and he was obliged to return to Leyden, nothing wiser than when he had left it.

On his arrival he hastened to the establishment from which Vanderhausen had hired the lumbering though, considering the times, most luxurious vehicle which the bridal party had employed to convey them to Rotterdam. From the driver of this machine he learned that, having proceeded by slow stages, they had late in the evening approached Rotterdam; but that before they entered the city, and while yet nearly a mile from it, a small party of men, soberly clad, and after the old fashion, with peaked beards and moustaches, standing in the centre of the road, obstructed the further progress of the carriage. The driver reined in his horses, much fearing, from the obscurity of the hour and the loneliness of the road, that some mischief was intended.

His fears were, however, somewhat allayed by him observing that these strange men carried a large litter of an antique shape, which they immediately set down upon the pavement, whereupon the bridegroom, having opened the coach-door from within, descended, and having assisted his bride to do likewise, led her, weeping bitterly and wringing her hands, to the litter, which they both entered. It was then raised by the men and speedily carried towards the city, and before it had proceeded many yards the darkness concealed it from the view of the Dutch charioteer.

In the insides of the vehicle he found a purse, whose contents more than thrice paid the hire of the carriage and man. He saw and could tell nothing more of Mynher Vanderhausen and the beautiful lady. This mystery was a source of deep anxiety and almost of grief to Gerard Douw.

There was evidently fraud in the dealing of Vanderhausen with him, though for what purpose committed he could not imagine. He greatly doubted how far it was possible for a man possessing in his countenance so strong an evidence of the presence of the most demoniac feelings, to be in reality anything but a villain, and every day that passed without his hearing from or of his niece, instead of inducing him to forget his fears, on the contrary tended more and more to exasperate them.

The loss of his niece's cheerful society tended also to depress his spirits; and in order to dispel this despondency, which often crept upon his mind after his daily employment was over, he was wont frequently to prevail upon Schalken to accompany him home, and by his presence to dispel, in some degree, the gloom of his otherwise solitary supper.

One evening, the painter and his pupil were sitting by the fire, having accomplished a comfortable supper, and had yielded to that silent pensiveness sometimes induced by the process of digestion, when their reflections were disturbed by a loud sound at the street-door, as if occasioned by some person rushing forcibly and repeatedly against it. A domestic had run without delay to ascertain the cause of the disturbance, and they heard him twice or thrice interrogate the applicant for admission, but without producing an answer or any cessation of the sounds.

They heard him then open the hall-door, and immediately there followed a light and rapid tread upon the staircase. Schalken laid his hand on his sword, and advanced towards the door. It opened before he reached it, and Rose rushed into the room. She looked wild and haggard, and pale with exhaustion and terror, but her dress surprised them as much even as her unexpected appearance. It consisted of a kind of white woollen wrapper, made close about the neck, and descending to the very ground. It was much deranged and travel-soiled. The poor creature had hardly entered the chamber when she fell senseless on the floor. With some difficulty they succeeded in reviving her, and on recovering her senses she instantly exclaimed, in a tone of eager, terrified impatience:

'Wine, wine, quickly, or I'm lost!'

Much alarmed at the strange agitation in which the call was made, they at once administered to her wishes, and she drank some wine with a haste and eagerness which surprised them. She had hardly swallowed it, when she exclaimed, with the same urgency:

'Food, food, at once, or I perish!'

A considerable fragment of a roast joint was upon the table, and Schalken immediately proceeded to cut some, but he was anticipated; for no sooner had she become aware of its presence than she darted at it with the rapacity of a vulture, and, seizing it in her hands she tore off the flesh with her teeth and swallowed it.

When the paroxysm of hunger had been a little appeased, she appeared suddenly to become aware how strange her conduct had been, or it may have been that other more agitating thoughts recurred to her mind, for she began to weep bitterly, and to wring her hands.

'Oh, send for a minister of God,' said she; 'I am not safe till he comes; send for him speedily.'

Gerard Douw despatched a messenger instantly, and prevailed on his niece to allow him to surrender his bedchamber to her use; he also persuaded her to retire to it at once and rest; her consent was extracted upon the condition that they would not leave her for a moment.

65

'Oh, that the holy man were here!' she said; 'he can deliver me. The dead and the living can never be one – God has forbidden it.'

With these mysterious words she surrendered herself to their guidance, and they proceeded to the chamber which Gerard Douw had assigned to her use.

'Do not – do not leave me for a moment,' said she. 'I am lost if you do.'

Gerard Douw's chamber was approached through a spacious apartment, which they were now about to enter. Gerard Douw and Schalken each carried a wax candle so that a sufficient degree of light was cast upon all surrounding objects. They were now entering the large chamber, which, as I have said, communicated with Douw's apartment, when Rose suddenly stopped, and, in a whisper which seemed to thrill with horror, she said:

'Oh, God! he is here – he is here! See, see – there he goes!'

She pointed towards the door of the inner room, and Schalken thought he saw a shadowy and ill-defined form gliding into that apartment. He drew his sword, and raising the candle so as to throw its light with increased distinction upon the objects in the room, he entered the chamber into which the shadow had glided. No figure was there – nothing but the furniture which belonged to the room, and yet he could not be deceived as to the fact that something had moved before them into the chamber.

A sickening dread came upon him, and the cold perspiration broke out in heavy drops upon his forehead; nor was he more composed when he heard the increased urgency, the agony of entreaty, with which Rose implored them not to leave her for a moment.

'I saw him,' said she. 'He's here! I cannot be deceived – I know him. He's by me – he's with me – he's in the room. Then, for God's sake, as you would save me, do not stir from beside me!'

They at length prevailed upon her to lie down upon the bed, where she continued to urge them to stay by her. She frequently uttered incoherent sentences, repeating again and again, 'The dead and the living cannot be one – God had forbidden it!' and then again, 'Rest to the wakeful – sleep to the sleep-walkers.'

These and other mysterious and broken sentences she continued to utter until the clergyman arrived.

Gerard Douw began to fear, naturally enough, that the poor girl, owing to terror or ill-treatment, had become deranged; and he half suspected, by the suddenness of her appearance, and the unreasonableness of the hour and, above all, from the wildness and terror of her manner, that she had made her escape from some place of confinement for lunatics, and was in immediate fear of pursuit. He resolved to summon medical advice as soon as the mind of his niece had been in some measure set at rest by the offices of the clergyman whose attendance she had so earnestly desired; and until this object had been attained, he did not venture to put any questions to her which might possibly, by reviving pitiful or horrible recollections, increase her agitation.

The clergyman soon arrived – a man of ascetic countenance and venerable age – one whom Gerard Douw respected much, forasmuch as he was a veteran polemic, though one, perhaps, more dreaded as a combatant than beloved as a Christian – of pure morality, subtle brain, and frozen heart. He entered the chamber which communicated with that in which Rose reclined, and immediately on his arrival she requested him to pray for her, as for one who lay in the hands of Satan, and who could hope for deliverance only from heaven.

That our readers may distinctly understand all the circumstances of the event which we are about imperfectly to describe, it is necessary to state the relative position of the parties who were engaged in it. The old clergyman and Schalken were in the anteroom of which we have already spoken; Rose lay in the inner chamber, the door of which was open; and by the side of the bed, at her urgent desire, stood her guardian; a candle burned in the bed-chamber, and three were lighted in the inner apartment.

The old man now cleared his voice, as if about to commence; but before he had time to begin, a sudden gust of air blew out the candle which served to illuminate the room in which the poor girl lay, and she, with hurried alarm, exclaimed:

'Godfrey, bring in another candle, the darkness is unsafe.'

Gerard Douw, forgetting for a moment her repeated injunctions in the immediate impulse, stepped from the bedchamber into the other, in order to supply what she desired.

'O God! do not go, dear uncle!' shrieked the unhappy girl; and at the same time she sprang from the bed and darted after him, in order, by her grasp, to detain him.

But the warning came too late, for scarcely had he passed the threshold, and hardly had his niece had time to utter the startling exclamation, when the door which divided the two rooms closed violently after him, as if swung by a strong blast of wind.

Schalken and he both rushed to the door, but their united and desperate efforts could not avail as much as to shake it.

Shriek after shriek burst forth from the inner chamber, with all the piercing loudness of despairing terror. Schalken and Douw applied every energy and strained every nerve to force open the door; but all in vain.

There was no sound of struggling within, but the screams seemed to increase in loudness, and at the same time they heard the bolts of the lattice window withdrawn, and the window itself grated upon the sill as if thrown open.

One last shriek, so long and piercing and agonised as to be scarcely human, swelled from the room, and suddenly there followed a death-like silence.

A light step was heard crossing the floor, as if from the bed to the window; and almost at the same instant the door gave way, and, yielding to the pressure of the external applicants, they were nearly precipitated into the room. It was empty. The window was open, and Schalken sprang to a chair and gazed out upon the street and the canal below. He saw no form, but he beheld, or thought he beheld, the waters of the broad canal beneath settling ring after ring in heavy circular ripples, as if a moment before disturbed by the immersion of some large and heavy mass.

No trace of Rose was ever after discovered, nor was anything certain respecting her mysterious wooer detected or even suspected; no clue whereby to trace the intricacies of the labyrinth and to arrive at a distinct conclusion was to be found. But an incident occurred, which, though it will not be received by our rational readers as at all approaching to evidence upon the matter, nevertheless produced a strong and lasting impression upon the mind of Schalken.

Many years after the events which we have detailed, Schalken, then remotely situated, received an intimation of his father's death, and of his intended burial upon a fixed day in the church of Rotterdam. It was necessary that a very considerable journey should be performed by the funeral procession, which, as it will readily be believed, was not very numerously attended. Schalken with difficulty arrived in Rotterdam late in the day upon which the funeral was appointed to take place. The procession had not then arrived. Evening closed in, and still it did not appear.

Schalken strolled down to the church. He found it open and notice of the funeral had been given, and the vault in which the body was to be laid had been opened. The official who corresponds to our sexton, on seeing a well-dressed gentleman whose object was to attend the expected funeral, pacing the aisle of the church, hospitably invited him to share with him the comforts of a blazing wood fire, which, as was his custom in winter time upon such occasions, he had kindled on the hearth of a chamber which communicated, by a flight of steps, with the vault below.

In this chamber Schalken and his entertainer seated themselves, and the sexton, after some fruitless attempts to engage his guest in conversation, was obliged to apply himself to his tobacco-pipe and can to solace his solitude.

In spite of his grief and cares, the fatigues of a rapid journey of nearly forty hours gradually overcame the mind and body of Godfrey Schalken, and he sank into a deep sleep, from which he was awakened by some one shaking him gently by the shoulder. He first thought that the old sexton had called him, but he was no longer in the room.

He roused himself, and as soon as he could clearly see what was around him, he perceived a female form, clothed in a kind of light robe of muslin, part of which was so disposed to act as a veil, and in her hand she carried a lamp. She was moving rather away from him, and towards the flight of steps which conducted towards the vaults.

Schalken felt a vague alarm at the sight of this figure, and at the same time an irresistible impulse to follow its guidance. He followed it towards the vaults, but when it reached the head of the stairs, he paused; the figure paused also, and, turning gently round, displayed, by the light of the lamp it carried, the face and featured of his first love, Rose Velderkaust. There was nothing horrible, or even sad, in the countenance. On the contrary, it wore the same sad smile which used to enchant the artist long before in his happy days.

A feeling of awe and interest, too intense to be resisted, prompted him to follow the spectre, if spectre it were. She descended the stairs – he followed; and, turning to the left, through a narrow passage, she led him, to his infinite surprise, into what appeared to be an old-fashioned Dutch apartment, such as the pictures of Gerard Douw have served to immortalise.

Abundance of costly antique furniture was disposed about the room, and in one corner stood a four-poster bed, with heavy black-cloth curtains around it; the figure frequently turned towards him with the same arch smile; and when she came to the side of the bed, she drew the curtains, and, by the light of the lamp which she held towards its contents, she disclosed to the horror-striken painter, sitting bolt upright in bed, the livid and demoniac form of Vanderhausen. Schalken had hardly seen him when he fell senseless upon the floor, where he lay until discovered, on the next morning, by persons employed in closing the passages into the vaults. He was lying in a cell of considerable size, which had not been disturbed for a long time, and he had fallen beside a large coffin which was supported upon small stone pillars, a security against the attacks of vermin.

To his dying day Schalken was satisfied of the reality of the vision which he had witnessed, and he has left behind him a curious evidence of the impression which it wrought upon his fancy, in a painting executed shortly after the event we have narrated, which is valuable as exhibiting not only the peculiarities which have made Schalken's pictures sought after, but even more so as presenting a portrait, as close and faithful as one taken from memory can be, of his early love, Rose Velderkaust, whose mysterious fate must ever remain a matter of speculation.

The picture represents a chamber of antique masonry, such as might be found in most old cathedrals, and is lighted faintly by a lamp carried in the hand of a female figure, such as we have above attempted to describe; and in the background, and to the left of him who examines the painting, there stands the form of a man apparently roused from sleep, and by his attitude, his hand being laid upon his sword, exhibiting considerable alarm: this last figure is illuminated only by the expiring glare of a wood or charcoal fire.

The whole production exhibits a beautiful specimen of that artful and singular distribution of light and shade which has rendered the name of Schalken immortal among the artists of his country. This tale is traditionary, and the reader will easily perceive, by our studiously omitting to heighten many points of the narrative, when a little additional colouring might have added effect to the recital, that we have desired to lay before him, not a figment of the brain, but a curious tradition connected with, and belonging to, the biography of a famous artist.

3
A Ghost Story

THOSE WHO REMEMBER Chapelizod a quarter of a century ago, or more, may possibly recollect the parish sexton. Bob Martin was held much in awe by truant boys who sauntered into the church-yard on Sundays, to read the tomb-stones, or play leap frog over them, or climb the ivy in search of bats' or sparrows' nests, or peep into the mysterious aperture under the eastern window, which opened a dim perspective of descending steps losing themselves among profounder darkness, where lidless coffins gaped horribly among tattered velvet, bones, and dust, which time and mortality had strewn there. Of such horribly curious, and otherwise enterprising juveniles, Bob was, of course, the special scourge and terror. But terrible as was the official aspect of the sexton, and repugnant as his lank form, clothed in musty, sable vesture, his small, frosty visage, suspicious grey eyes, and rusty, brown scratch-wig, might appear to all notions of genial frailty, it was yet true, that Bob Martin's severe morality sometimes nodded, and that Bacchus did not always solicit him in vain.

Bob had a curious mind, a memory well stored with 'merry tales', and tales of terror. His profession familiarised him with graves and goblins, and his tastes with weddings, wassail, and sly frolics of all sorts. And as his personal recollections ran back nearly three score years into the perspective of village history, his fund of local anecdotes was copious, accurate, and edifying.

As his ecclesiastical revenues were by no means considerable, he was not unfrequently obliged, for the indulgences of his tastes, to arts which were, at the best, undignified.

He frequently invited himself when his entertainers had forgotten to do so; he dropped in accidentally upon small drinking parties of his acquaintance in public houses, and entertained them with stories, queer or terrible, from his inexhaustible reservoir, never scrupling to accept an acknowledgment in the shape of hot whiskey punch or whatever else was going.

There was at that time a certain atrabilious publican called Philip Slaney, established in a shop nearly opposite the old turnpike. This man was not, when left to himself, immoderately given to drinking; but being naturally of a saturnine complexion, and his spirits constantly requiring a fillip, he acquired a prodigious liking for Bob Martin's company. The sexton's society, in fact, gradually became the solace of his existence, and he seemed to lose his constitutional melancholy in the fascination of his sly jokes and marvellous stories.

This intimacy did not redound to the prosperity or reputation of the convivial allies. Bob Martin drank a good deal more punch that was good for his health, or consistent with the character of an ecclesiastical functionary. Philip Slaney, too, was drawn into similar indulgencies, for it was hard to resist the genial seductions of his gifted companion; and as he was obliged to pay for both, his purse was believed to have suffered even more than his head and liver.

Be this as it may, Bob Martin had the credit of having made a drunkard of 'black Phil Slaney' – for by this cognomen was he distinguished; and Phil

Slaney had also the reputation of having made the sexton, if possible, a 'bigger bliggard' than ever. Under the circumstances, the accounts of the concern opposite the turnpike became somewhat entangled; and it came to pass one drowsy summer morning, the weather being at once sultry and cloudy, that Phil Slaney went into a small back parlour where he kept his books, and which commanded, through its dirty window-panes, a full view of a dead wall, and having bolted the door, he took a loaded pistol, and clapping the muzzle to his mouth, blew the upper part of his skull through the ceiling.

This horrid catastrophe shocked Bob Martin extremely; and partly on this account, and partly because having been, on several late occasions, found at night in a state of abstraction, bordering on insensibility, upon the high road, he had been threatened with dismissal; and, as some said, partly also because of the difficulty of finding anybody to 'treat' him as poor Phil Slaney used to do, he for a time foreswore alcohol in all its combinations, and became an eminent example of temperance and sobriety.

Bob observed his good resolutions, greatly to the comfort of his wife, and the edification of the neighbourhood, with tolerable punctuality. He was seldom tipsy, and never drunk, and was greeted by the better part of society with the honours of the prodigal son.

Now it happened, about a year after the grisly event we have mentioned, that the curate having received, by the post, due notice of a funeral to be consummated in the churchyard of Chapelizod, with

78

'... The traveller was acknowledged by all to have been the spectre of the suicide ...'

(see p. 85)

certain instructions respecting the site of the grave, despatched a summons to Bob Martin, with a view to communicate to that functionary these official details.

It was a lowering autumn night: piles of lurid thunder-clouds slowly rising from the earth, had loaded the sky with a solemn and boding canopy of storm. The growl of the distant thunder was heard afar off upon the dull, still air, and all nature seemed, as it were, hushed and cowering under the oppressive influence of the approaching tempest.

It was past nine o'clock when Bob, putting on his official coat of seedy black, prepared to attend his professional superior.

'Bobby, darlin',' said his wife, before she delivered the hat she held in her hand to his keeping, 'sure you won't, Bobby, darlin' – you won't – you know what.'

'I *don't* know what,' he retorted, smartly, grasping at his hat.

'You won't be throwing up the little finger, Bobby, acushla?' she said, evading his grasp.

'Arrah, why would I, woman? There, give me my hat, will you?'

'But won't you promise me, Bobby darlin' – won't you, alanna?'

'Ay, ay, to be sure I will – why not? – there, give me my hat, and let me go.'

'Ay, but you're not promisin', Bobby, mavourneen, you're not promisin' all the time.'

'Well, divil carry me if I drink a drop till I come back again,' said the sexton, angrily; 'will that do you? And *now* will you give me my hat?'

'Here it is, darlin',' she said, 'and God send you safe back.'

And with this parting blessing she closed the door upon his retreating figure, for it was now quite dark, and resumed her knitting till his return, very much relieved; for she thought that he had of late been oftener tipsy than was consistent with his thorough reformation, and feared the allurements of the half dozen 'publics' which he had at that time to pass on his way to the other end of the town.

They were still open, and exhaled a delicious reek of whiskey, as Bob glided wistfully by them; but he stuck his hands in his pockets and looked the other way, whistling resolutely, and filling his mind with the image of the curate and anticipations of his coming fee. Thus he steered his morality safely through these rocks of offence, and reached the curate's lodging in safety.

He had, however, an unexpected sick call to attend, and was not at home, so that Bob Martin had to sit in the hall and amuse himself with the devil's tattoo until his return. This, unfortunately, was very long delayed, and it must have been fully twelve o'clock when Bob Martin set out upon his homeward way. By this time the storm had gathered to a pitchy darkness, the bellowing thunder was heard among the rocks and hollows of the Dublin mountains, and the pale, blue lightning shone upon the staring fronts of the houses.

By this time, too, every door was closed; but as Bob trudged homeward, his eye mechanically sought the public-house which had once belonged to Phil

Slaney. A faint light was making its way through the shutters and the glass panes over the doorway, which made a sort of dull, foggy halo about the front of the house.

As Bob's eyes had become accustomed to the obscurity by this time, the light in question was quite sufficient to enable him to see a man in a sort of loose riding-coat seated upon a bench which, at that time, was fixed under the window of the house. He wore his hat very much over his eyes, and was smoking a long pipe. The outline of a glass and a quart bottle was also dimly traceable beside him; and a large horse saddled, but faintly discernible, was patiently awaiting his master's leisure.

There was something odd, no doubt, in the appearance of a traveller refreshing himself at such an hour in the open street; but the sexton accounted for it easily by supposing that, on the closing of the house for the night, he had taken what remained of his refection to the place where he was now discussing it al fresco.

At another time Bob might have saluted the stranger as he passed with a friendly 'good night', but, somehow, he was out of humour and in no genial mood, and was about passing without any courtesy of the sort, when the stranger, without taking the pipe from his mouth, raised the bottle, and with it beckoned him familiarly while, with a sort of lurch of the head and shoulders, and at the same time shifting his seat to the end of the bench, he pantomimically invited him to share his seat and his cheer. There was a divine fragrance of whiskey about the spot, and

82

Bob half relented; but he remembered his promise just as he began to waver, and said:

'No, I thank you sir; I can't stop to-night.'

The stranger beckoned with vehement welcome, and pointed to the vacant space on the seat beside him.

'I thank you for your polite offer,' said Bob, 'but it's what I'm too late as it is, and haven't time to spare, so I wish you a good night.'

The traveller jingled the glass against the neck of the bottle, as if to intimate that he might at least swallow a dram without losing time. Bob was mentally quite of the same opinion; but, though his mouth watered, he remembered his promise, and shaking his head with incorruptible resolution, walked on.

The stranger, pipe in mouth, rose from his bench, the bottle in one hand, and the glass in the other, and followed at the sexton's heels, his dusky horse keeping close in his wake.

There was something suspicious and unaccountable in this importunity.

Bob quickened his pace, but the stranger followed close. The sexton began to feel queer, and turned about. His pursuer was behind, and still inviting him with impatient gestures to taste his liquor.

'I told you before,' said Bob, who was both angry and frightened, 'that I would not taste it, and that's enough. I don't want to have anything to say to you or your bottle; and in God's name,' he added, still more vehemently, observing that he was approaching still close, 'fall back and don't be tormenting me this way.'

These words, as it seemed, incensed the stranger, for he shook the bottle with violent menace at Bob Martin; but, notwithstanding this gesture of defiance, he suffered the distance between them to increase. Bob, however, beheld him dogging him still in the distance, for his pipe shed a wonderful red glow, which duskily illuminated his entire figure like the lurid atmosphere of a meteor.

'I wish the devil had his own, my boy,' muttered the excited sexton, 'and I know well enough where you'd be.'

The next time he looked over his shoulder, to his dismay, he observed the importunate stranger as close as ever upon his track.

'Confound you,' cried the man of skulls and shovels, almost beside himself with rage and horror, 'what is it you want of me?'

The stranger appeared more confident, and kept wagging his head and extending both glass and bottle towards him as he drew near, and Bob Martin heard the horse snorting as it followed in the dark.

'Keep it to yourself, whatever it is, for there is neither grace nor luck about you,' cried Bob Martin, freezing with terror; 'leave me alone, will you.'

And he fumbled in vain among the seething confusion of his ideas for a prayer or an exorcism. He quickened his pace almost to a run; he was now close to his own door, under the impending bank by the river side.

'Let me in, let me in, for God's sake; Molly, open the door,' he cried, as he ran to the threshold, and leant his back against the plank. His pursuer confronted him upon the road; the pipe was no longer in his mouth, but the dusky red glow still lingered round him. He uttered some inarticulate cavernous sounds, which were wolfish and indescribable, while he seemed employed in pouring out a glass from the bottle.

The sexton kicked with all his force against the door, and cried at the same time with a despairing voice.

'In the name of God Almighty, once for all, leave me alone.'

His pursuer furiously flung the contents of the bottle at Bob Martin; but instead of fluid it issued out in a stream of flame, which expanded and whirled round them, and for a moment they were both enveloped in a faint blaze; at the same instant a sudden gust whisked off the stranger's hat, and the sexton beheld that his skull was roofless. For an instant he beheld the gaping aperture, black and shattered, and then he fell senseless into his own doorway, which his affrighted wife had just unbarred.

I need hardly give my reader the key to this most intelligible and authentic narrative. The traveller was acknowledged by all to have been the spectre of the suicide, called up by the Evil One to tempt the convivial sexton into a violation of his promise, sealed, as it was, by an imprecation. Had he succeeded, no doubt the dusky steed, which Bob had seen saddled in attendance, was destined to have carried back a double burden to the place from whence it came.

As an attestation of the reality of this visitation, the old thorn tree which overhung the doorway was found in the morning to have been blasted with the infernal fires which had issued from the bottle, just as if a thunderbolt has scorched it.

4
A Haunted House

WITHIN THE LAST eight years – the precise date I purposely omit – I was ordered by my physician, my health being in an unsatisfactory state, to change my residence to one upon the sea-coast; and accordingly, I took a house for a year in a fashionable watering-place, at a moderate distance from the city in which I had previously resided, and connected with it by a railway.

Winter was setting in when my removal thither was decided upon; but there was nothing whatever dismal or depressing in the change. The house I had taken was to all appearance, and in point of convenience, too, quite a modern one. It formed one in a cheerful row, with small gardens in front, facing the sea, and commanding sea air and sea views in perfection. In the rear it had coach-house and stable, and between them and the house a considerable grass-plot, with some flower-beds, interposed.

Our family consisted of my wife and myself, with three children, the eldest about nine years old, she and the next in age being girls; and the youngest, between six and seven, a boy. To these were added six servants, whom, although for certain reasons I decline giving their real names. I shall indicate, for the sake of clearness, by arbitrary ones. There was a nurse, Mrs Southerland; a nursery-maid, Ellen Page; the cook, Mrs Greenwood; and the housemaid, Ellen Faith; a butler, whom I shall call Smith, and his son, James, about two-and-twenty.

We came out to take possession at about seven o'clock in the evening; every thing was comfortable and cheery; good fires lighted, the rooms neat and airy, and a general air of preparation and comfort, highly conducive to good spirits and pleasant anticipations.

The sitting-rooms were large and cheerful, and they and the bed-rooms more than ordinarily lofty, the kitchen and servants' rooms, on the same level, were well and comfortably furnished, and had, like the rest of the house, an air of recent painting and fitting up, and a completely modern character, which imparted a very cheerful air of cleanliness and convenience.

There had been just enough of the fuss of settling agreeably to occupy us, and to give a pleasant turn to our thoughts after we had retired to our rooms. Being an invalid, I had a small bed to myself – resigning the four-poster to my wife. The candle was extinguished, but a night-light was burning. I was coming up stairs, and she, already in bed, had just dismissed her maid, when we were both startled by a wild scream from her room; I found her in a state of the extremest agitation and terror. She insisted that she had seen an unnaturally tall figure come beside her bed and stand there. The light was too faint to enable her to define any thing respecting this apparition, beyond the fact of her having most distinctly seen such a shape, colourless from the insufficiency of the light to disclose more than its dark outline.

We both endeavoured to reassure her. The room once more looked so cheerful in the candlelight, that we were quite uninfluenced by the contagion of her terrors. The movements and voices of the servants down stairs still getting things into their places and completing our comfortable arrangements, had also their effect in steeling us against any such influence, and we set the whole thing down as a dream, or an imperfectly-seen outline of the bed-curtains. When, however, we were alone, my wife reiterated, still in great agitation, her clear assertion that she had most positively seen, being at the time as completely awake as ever she was, precisely what she had described to us. And in this conviction she continued perfectly firm.

A day or two after this, it came out that our servants were under an apprehension that, somehow or other, thieves had established a secret mode of access to the lower part of the house. The butler, Smith, had seen an ill-looking woman in his room on the first night of our arrival; and he and other servants constantly saw, for many days subsequently, glimpses of a retreating figure, which corresponded with that so seen by him, passing through a passage which led to a back area in which were some coal-vaults.

This figure was seen always in the act of retreating, its back turned, generally getting round the corner of the passage into the area, in a stealthy and hurried way, and when closely followed, imperfectly seen again entering one of the coal-vaults, and when pursued into it, nowhere to be found.

The idea of any thing supernatural in the matter had, strange to say, not yet entered the mind of any one of the servants. They had heard some stories of smugglers having secret passages into houses, and using their means of access for purposes of pillage, or with a view to frighten superstitious people out of houses which they needed for their own objects, and a suspicion of similar practices here, caused them extreme uneasiness. The apparent anxiety also manifested by this retreating figure to escape observation, and her always appearing to make her egress at the same point, favoured this romantic hypothesis. The men, however, made a most careful examination of the back area, and of the coal-vaults, with a view to discover some mode of egress, but entirely without success. On the contrary, the result was, so far as it went, subversive of the theory; solid masonry met them on every hand.

I called the man, Smith, up, to hear from his own lips the particulars of what he had seen; and certainly his report was very curious. I give it as literally as my memory enables me:

His son slept in the same room, and was sound asleep; but he lay awake, as men sometimes will on a change of bed, and having many things on his mind. He was lying with his face towards the wall, but observing a light and some little stir in the room, he turned round in his bed, and saw the figure of a woman, squalid, and ragged in dress; her figure rather low and broad; as well as I recollect, she had something – either cloak or shawl – on, and wore a bonnet. Her back was turned, and she appeared to be searching or rummaging for something on the floor, and, without appearing to observe him, she turned in doing so towards him. The light, which was more like the intense glow of a coal, as he described it, being of a deep red colour, proceeded from the hollow of her hand, which she held beside her head, and he saw her perfectly distinctly. She appeared middle-aged, was deeply pitted with the smallpox, and blind of one eye. His phrase in describing her general appearance was, that she was 'a miserable, poor-looking creature.'

He was under the impression that she must be the woman who had been left by the proprietor in charge of the house, and who had that evening, after having given up the keys, remained for some little time with the female servants.

He coughed, therefore, to apprise her of his presence, and turned again towards the wall. When he again looked around she and the light were gone; and odd as was her method of lighting herself in her search, the circumstances excited neither uneasiness nor curiosity in his mind, until he discovered next morning that the woman in question had left the house long before he had gone to his bed.

I examined the man very closely as to the appearance of the person who had visited him, and the result was what I have described. It struck me as an odd thing, that even then, considering how prone to superstition persons in his rank of life usually are, he did not seem to suspect any thing supernatural in the occurrence; and, on the contrary, was thoroughly persuaded that his visitant was a living person, who had got into the house by some hidden entrance.

On Sunday, on his return from his place of worship, he told me that, when the service was ended, and the congregation making their way slowly out, he saw the very woman in the crowd, and kept his eye upon her for several minutes, but such was the crush, that all his efforts to reach her were unavailing, and when he got into the open street she was gone. He was quite positive as to his having distinctly seen her, however, for several minutes, and scouted the possibility of any mistake as to identity; and fully impressed with the substantial and living reality of his visitant, he was very much provoked at her having escaped him. He made inquiries also in the neighbourhood, but could procure no information, nor hear of any other persons having seen any woman corresponding with his description.

The cook and housemaid occupied a bedroom on the kitchen floor. It had whitewashed walls, and they were actually terrified by the appearance of the shadow of a woman passing and repassing across the side wall opposite to their beds. They suspected that this had been going on much longer than they were aware, for its presence was discovered by a sort of accident, its movements happening to take a direction in distinct contrariety to theirs.

This shadow always moved upon one particular wall, returning after short intervals, and causing them extreme terror. They placed the candle, as the most obvious specific, so close to the infested wall, that the flame all but touched it; and believed for some time that they had effectually got rid of this annoyance; but one night, notwithstanding this arrangement of the light, the shadow returned, passing and repassing, as heretofore, upon the same wall, although their only candle was burning within an inch of it, and it was obvious that no substance capable of casting such a shadow could have interposed; and, indeed as they described it, the shadow seemed to have no sort of relation to the position of the light, and appeared, as I have said, in manifest defiance of the law of optics.

I ought to mention that the housemaid was a particularly fearless sort of person, as well as a very honest one; and her companion, the cook, a scrupulously religious woman, and both agreed in every particular in their relation of what occurred.

Meanwhile, the nursery was not without its annoyances, though as yet of a comparatively trivial kind.

Sometimes, at night, the handle of the door was turned hurriedly as if by a person trying to come in, and at others a knocking was made at it. These sounds occurred after the children had settled to sleep, and while the nurse still remained awake. Whenever she called to know 'who is there,' the sounds ceased; but several times, and particularly at first, she was under the impression that they were caused by her mistress, who had come to see the children, and thus impressed she had got up and opened the door, expecting to see her, but discovering only darkness, and receiving no answer to her inquiries.

With respect to this nurse, I must mention that I believe no more perfectly trustworthy servant was ever employed in her capacity; and, in addition to her integrity, she was remarkably gifted with sound common sense.

One morning, I think about three or four weeks after our arrival, I was sitting at the parlour window which looked to the front, when I saw the little iron door which admitted into the small garden that lay between the window where I was sitting and the public road, pushed open by a woman who so exactly answered the description given by Smith of the woman who had visited his room on the night of his arrival as instantaneously to impress me with the conviction that she must be the identical person. She was a square, short woman, dressed in soiled and tattered clothes, scarred and pitted with small-pox, and blind of an eye. She stepped hurriedly into the little enclosure, and peered from a distance of a few yards into the room where I was sitting.

I felt that now was the moment to clear the matter up; but there was something stealthy in the manner and look of the woman which convinced me that I must not appear to notice her until her retreat was fairly cut off. Unfortunately, I was suffering from a lame foot, and could not reach the bell as quickly as I wished. I made all the haste I could, and rang violently to bring up the servant Smith. In the short interval that intervened, I observed the woman from the window, who having in a leisurely way, and with a kind of scrutiny, looked along the front windows of the house, passed quickly out again, closing the gate after her, and followed a lady who was walking along the footpath at a quick pace, as if with the intention of begging from her.

The moment the man entered I told him: 'The blind woman you described to me has this instant followed a lady in that direction; try to overtake her.' He was, if possible, more eager than I in the chase, but returned in a short time after a vain pursuit, very hot, and utterly disappointed. And, thereafter, we saw her face no more.

All this time, and up to the period of our leaving the house, which was not for two or three months later, there occurred at intervals the only phenomenon in the entire series having any resemblance to what we hear described of 'Spiritualism'. This was a knocking, like a soft hammering with a wooden mallet, as it seemed in the timbers between the bedroom ceilings and the roof. It had this special peculiarity, that it was always rhythmical and, I think, invariably, the emphasis upon the last stroke.

It would sound rapidly 'one, two, three, *four* – one, two, three, *four*'. or 'one, two, *three* – one, two, *three*.' and sometimes 'one, *two* – one, *two*.' etcetera, and this, with intervals and resumptions, monotonously for hours at a time.

At first this caused my wife, who was a good deal confined to her bed, much annoyance; and we sent to our neighbours to inquire if any hammering or capentering was going on in their houses, but were informed that nothing of the sort was taking place. I have myself heard it frequently, always in the same inaccessible part of the house, amd with the same monotonous emphasis. One odd thing about it was, that on my wife's calling out, as she used to do when it became more than usually troublesome, 'stop that noise,' it was invariably arrested for a longer or shorter time.

Of course none of these occurrences was ever mentioned in hearing of the children. They would have been, no doubt, like most children, greatly terrified had they heard anything of the matter, and

'. . . grubbed up a jawbone with several teeth in it . . .' (see p. 104)

known that their elders were unable to account for what was passing; and their fears would have made them wretched and troublesome.

They used to play for some hours every day in the back garden – the house forming one end of this oblong inclosure, the stable and coach-house the other, and two parallel walls of considerable height the sides. Here, as it afforded a perfectly safe playground, they were frequently left quite to themselves; and in talking over their day's adventures, as children will, they happened to mention a woman, or rather the woman, for they had long grown familiar with her appearance, whom they used to see in the garden while they were at play.

They assumed that she came in and went out at the stable door, but they never actually saw her enter or depart. They merely saw a figure – that of a very poor woman, soiled and ragged – near the stable wall, stooping over the ground, and apparently grubbing in the loose clay in search of something. She did not disturb, or appear to observe them; and they left her in undisturbed possession of her nook of ground. When seen it was always in the same spot, and similarly occupied; and the description they gave of her general appearance – for they never saw her face – corresponded with that of the one-eyed woman whom Smith, and subsequently as it seemed, I had seen.

The other man, James, who looked after a mare which I had purchased for the purpose of riding exercise, had, like every one else in the house, his little trouble to report, though it was not much. The stall in which, as the most comfortable, it was decided to place her, she peremptorily declined to enter. Though a very docile and gentle little animal, there was no getting her into it. She would snort and rear, and, in fact, do or suffer anything rather than set her hoof in it. He was fain, therefore, to place her in another. And on several occasions he found her there, exhibiting all the equine symptoms of extreme fear.

Like the rest of us, however, this man was not troubled in the particular case with any superstitious qualms. The mare had evidently been frightened; and he was puzzled to find out how, or by whom, for the stable was well-secured, and had, I am nearly certain, a lock-up yard outside.

One morning I was greeted with the intelligence that robbers had certainly got into the house in the night; and that one of them had actually been seen in the nursery.

The witness, I found, was my eldest child, then, as I have said, about nine years of age. Having awoke in the night, and lain awake for some time in her bed, she heard the handle of the door turn, and a person whom she distinctly saw – for it was a light night, and the window-shutters unclosed – but whom she had never seen before, stepped in on tiptoe, and with an appearance of great caution. He was a rather small man, with a very red face; he wore an oddly cut frock coat, the collar of which stood up, and trousers, rough and wide, like those of a sailor, turned up at the ankles, and either short boots or clumsy shoes, covered with mud.

This man listened beside the nurse's bed, which

stood next the door, as if to satisfy himself that she was sleeping soundly; and having done so for some seconds, he began to move cautiously in a diagonal line, across the room to the chimney-piece, where he stood for a while, and so resumed his tiptoe walk, skirting the wall, until he reached a chest of drawers, some of which were open, and into which he looked, and began to rummage in a hurried way, as the child supposed, making search for something worth taking away.

He then passed on to the window, where was a dressing-table, at which he also stopped, turning over the things upon it, and standing for some time at the window as if looking out, and then resuming his walk by the side wall opposite to that by which he had moved up to the window, he returned in the same way toward the nurse's bed, so as to reach it at the foot.

With its side to the end wall, in which was the door, was placed the little bed in which lay my eldest child, who watched his proceedings with the extremest terror. As he drew near she instinctively movèd herself in the bed, with her head and shoulders to the wall, drawing up her feet; but he passed by without appearing to observe, or, at least, to care for her presence. Immediately after the nurse turned in her bed as if about to waken; and when the child, who had drawn the clothes about her head, again ventured to peep out, the man was gone.

The child had no idea of her having seen any thing more formidable than a thief. With the prowling, cautious, and noiseless manner of proceeding common to such marauders, the air and movements of the man whom she had seen entirely corresponded. And on hearing her perfectly distinct and consistent account, I could myself arrive at no other conclusion than that a stranger had actually got into the house.

I had, therefore, in the first instance, a most careful examination made to discover any traces of an entrance having been made by any window into the house. The doors had been found barred and locked as usual; but no sign of any thing of the sort was discernible. I then had the various articles – plate, wearing apparel, books, etcetera, counted; and after having conned over and reckoned up every thing, it became quite clear that nothing whatever had been removed from the house, nor was there the slightest indication of any thing having been so much as disturbed there. I must here state that this child was remarkably clear, intelligent, and observant; and that her description of the man, and of all that had occurred, was most exact, and as detailed as the want of perfect light rendered possible.

I felt assured that an entrance had actually been effected into the house, though for what purpose was not easily to be conjectured.

The man, Smith, was equally confident upon this point; and his theory was that the object was simply to frighten us out of the house by making us believe it haunted; and he was more than ever anxious and on the alert to discover the conspirators.

It often since appeared to me odd. Every year, indeed, more odd, as this cumulative case of the marvellous becomes to my mind more and more inexplicable – that underlying my sense of mystery and puzzle, was all along the quiet assumption that all these occurrences were one way or another referable to natural causes. I could not account for them, indeed, myself; but during the whole period I inhabited that house, I never once felt, though much alone, and often up very late at night, any of those tremors and thrills which every one has at times experienced when situation and the hour are favourable. Except the cook and housemaid, who were plagued with the shadow I mentioned crossing and recrossing upon the bedroom wall, we all, without exception, experienced the same strange sense of security, and regarded these phenomena rather with a perplexed sort of interest and curiosity, than with any more unpleasant sensations.

The knockings which I have mentioned at the nursery door, preceded generally by the sound of a step on the lobby, meanwhile continued. At that time (for my wife, like myself, was an invalid) two eminent physicians, who came out occasionally by rail, were attending us. These gentlemen were at first only amused, but ultimately interested, and very much puzzled by the occurrences which we described. One of them, at last, recommended that a candle should be kept burning upon the lobby. It was in fact a recurrence to an old woman's recipe against ghosts – of course it might be serviceable too, against imposters; at all events, seeming, as I have said, very much interested and puzzled, he advised it, and it was tried. We fancied that it was successful; for there was an interval of quiet for, I think, three or four nights.

But after that, the noises – the footsteps on the lobby, the knocking at the door, and the turning of the handle recommenced in full force, notwithstanding the light upon the table outside; and these particular phenomena became only more perplexing than ever.

The alarm of robbers and smugglers gradually subsided after a week or two; but we were again to hear news from the nursery. Our second little girl, then between seven and eight years of age, saw in the night time – she alone being awake – a young woman, with black, or very dark hair, which hung loose, and with a black cloak on, standing near the middle of the floor, opposite the hearth-stone, and fronting the foot of her bed. She appeared quite unobservant of the children and nurse sleeping in the room. She was very pale, and looked, the child said, both 'sorry and frightened', and with something very peculiar and terrible about her eyes, which made the child conclude that she was dead. She was looking, not at, but in, the direction of the child's bed, and there was a dark streak across her throat, like a scar with blood upon it. This figure was not motionless; but once or twice turned slowly, and without appearing to be conscious of the presence of the child, or the other occupants of the room, like a person in vacancy or abstraction.

There was on this occasion a night-light burning in the chamber; and the child saw, or thought she saw, all these particulars with the utmost distinctness. She got her head under the bed-clothes; and although a good many years have passed since then, she cannot recall the spectacle without feelings of peculiar horror.

One day, when the children were playing in the back garden, I asked them to point out to me the spot where they were accustomed to see the woman who occasionally showed herself as I have described, near the stable wall. There was no division of opinion as to this precise point, which they indicated in the most distinct and confident way. I suggested that, perhaps, something might be hidden there in the ground; and advised them digging a hole there with their little spades, to try for it. Accordingly, to work they went, and by my return in the evening they had grubbed up a piece of jawbone, with several teeth in it. The bone was very much decayed, and ready to crumble to pieces, but the teeth were quite sound. I could not tell whether they were human grinders; but I showed the fossil to one of the physicians I have mentioned, who came out the next evening, and he pronounced them human teeth. The same conclusion was come to a day or two later by the other medical man.

It appears to me now, on reviewing the whole matter, almost unaccountable that, with such evidence before me, I should not have got in a labourer, and had the spot effectually dug and searched. I can only say, that so it was. I was quite satisfied of the moral truth of every word that had been related to me, and which I have here set down with scrupulous accuracy.

But I experienced an apathy, for which neither then nor afterwards did I quite know how to account. I had a vague, but immovable impression that the whole affair was referable to natural agencies. It was not until some time after we had left the house,

which, by-the-by, we afterwards found had the
reputation of being haunted before we had come to
live in it, that on reconsideration I discovered the
serious difficulty of accounting satisfactorily for all
that had occurred upon ordinary principles.

A great deal we might arbitrarily set down to
imagination. But even in so doing there was, *in
limine,* the oddity, not to say improbability, of so
many different persons having nearly simultaneously
suffered from different spectral and other illusions
during the short period for which we had occupied
that house, who never before, nor so far as we
learned, afterwards were troubled by any fears or
fancies of the sort. There were other things too, not
to be so accounted for. The odd knockings in the roof
I frequently heard myself.

There were also, which I before forgot to mention,
in the daytime, rappings at the doors of the sitting-
rooms, which constantly deceived us; and it was not
till our 'come in' was unanswered, and the hall or
passage outside the door was discovered to be empty,
that we learned that whatever else caused them,
human hands did not. All the persons who reported
having seen the different persons or appearances here
described by me, were just as confident of having
literally and distinctly seen them, as I was of having
seen the hard-featured woman with the blind eye, so
remarkably corresponding with Smith's description.

About a week after the discovery of the teeth,
which were found, I think, about two feet under the
ground, a friend, much advanced in years, who
remembered the town in which we had now taken up

our abode, for a very long time, happened to pay us a visit He good-humourediy pooh-poohed the whole thing; but at the same time was evidently curious about it.

'We might construct a sort of story,' said I (I am giving, of course, the substance and purport, not the exact words, of our dialogue), 'and assign to each of the three figures who appeared their respective parts in some dreadful tragedy enacted in this house. The male figure represents the murderer; the ill-looking, one-eyed woman his accomplice, who, we will suppose, buried the body where she is now so often seen grubbing in the earth, and where the human teeth and jawbone have so lately been disinterred; and the young woman with dishevelled tresses, and black cloak, and the bloody scar across her throat, their victim. A difficulty, however, which I cannot get over, exists in the cheerfulness, the great publicity, and the evident very recent date of the house.'

'Why, as to that,' said he, 'the house is *not* modern; it and those beside it formed an old government store, altered and fitted up recently as you see. I remember it well in my young days, fifty years ago, before the town had grown out in this direction, and a more entirely lonely spot, or one more fitted for the commission of a secret crime, could not have been imagined.'

I have nothing to add, for very soon after this my physician pronounced a longer stay unnecessary for my health, and we took our departure for another place of abode. I may add, that, although I have resided for considerable periods in many other houses, I never experienced any annoyances of a similar kind elsewhere; neither have I made (stupid dog! you will say) any inquiries respecting either the antecedents or subsequent history of the house in which we made so disturbed a sojourn. I was content with what I knew, and have here related as clearly as I could, and I think it a very pretty puzzle as it stands.

5
My Uncle Watson

A VERY ODD thing happened to my uncle, Mr Watson, of Haddlestone; and to enable you to understand it, I must begin at the beginning.

In the year 1822, Mr James Walshawe, more commonly known as Captain Walshawe, died at the age of eighty-one years. The Captain in his early days, and so long as health and strength permitted, was a scamp of the active, intriguing sort; and spent his days and nights in sowing wild oats, of which he seemed to have an inexhaustible stock. The harvest of this village was plentifully interspersed with thorns, nettles, and thistles, which stung the husbandman unpleasantly, and did not enrich him.

Captain Walshawe was very well known in the neighbourhood of Wauling, and very generally avoided there. A 'captain' by courtesy, for he had never reached that rank in the army list. He had quitted the service in 1766, at the age of twenty-five; immediately previous to which period his debts had grown so troublesome, that he was induced to extricate himself by running away and marrying an heiress.

Though not so wealthy quite as he had imagined, she proved a very comfortable instrument for what remained of his shattered affections; and he lived and enjoyed himself very much in his odd way, upon her income, getting into no end of escapades and scandals, and a good deal of debt and money trouble.

When he married his wife, he was quartered in Ireland, at Clonmel, where was a nunnery, in which, as pensioner, resided Miss O'Neill, or as she was called in the country, Peg O'Neill – the heiress of whom I have spoken.

110

Her situation was the only ingredient of romance in the affair, for the young lady was decidedly plain, though good-humoured looking, with that style of features which is termed potato; and in figure she was a little too plump, and rather short. But she was impressible; and the handsome young English lieutenant was too much for her monastic tendencies, and she eloped.

In England there are traditions of Irish fortune-hunters, and in Ireland of English. The fact is, it was the vagrant class of each country that chiefly visited the other in old times, and a handsome vagabond, whether at home or abroad, I suppose, made the most of his face, which was also his fortune.

At all events, he carried off the fair one from the sanctuary; and for some sufficient reason, I suppose, they took up their abode at Wauling, in Lancashire.

Here the gallant captain amused himself after his fashion, sometimes running up, of course on business, to London. I believe few wives have ever cried more in a given time than did the poor, dumpy, potato-faced heiress, who got over the nunnery wall, and jumped into the handsome Captain's arms, for love.

He spent her fortune, frightened her out of her wits with oaths and threats, and broke her heart.

Latterly she shut herself up pretty nearly altogether in her room. She had an old, rather grim, Irish servant-woman in attendance upon her. This domestic was tall, lean, and religious, and the Captain knew instinctively she hated him; and he hated her in return, and often threatened to put her out of the house, and sometimes even to kick her out

111

of the window. And whenever a wet day confined him to the house or the stable, and he grew tired of smoking, he would begin to swear and curse at her for a diddled old mischief-maker, that could never be easy, and was always troubling the house with her cursed stories, and so forth.

But years passed away, and old Molly Doyle remained still in her original position. Perhaps he thought that there must be somebody there, and that he was not, after all, very likely to change for the better.

2.

He tolerated another intrusion, too, and thought himself a paragon of patience and easy good-nature for so doing. A Roman Catholic clergyman, in a long black frock, with a low standing collar, and a little white muslin fillet round his neck – tall, sallow, with blue chin, and dark steady eyes – used to glide up and down the stairs, and through the passages; and the Captain sometimes met him in one place and sometimes in another. But by a caprice incident to such tempers he treated this cleric exceptionally, and even with a surly sort of courtesy, though he grumbled about his visits behind his back.

I do not know that he had a great deal of moral courage, and the ecclesiastic looked severe and self-possessed; and somehow he thought he had no good opinion of him, and if a natural occasion were offered might say extremely unpleasant things, and hard to be answered.

Well the time came at last, when poor Peg O'Neill – in an evil hour Mrs James Walshawe – must cry, and quake, and pray her last. The doctor came from Penlynden, and was just as vague as usual, but more gloomy, and for about a week came and went oftener. The cleric in the long black frock was also daily there. And at last came that last sacrament in the gates of death, when the sinner is traversing those dread steps that never can be retraced; when the face is turned for ever from life, and we see a receding shape, and hear a voice already irrevocably in the land of spirits.

So the poor lady died; and some people said the Captain 'felt it very much'. I don't think he did. But he was not very well just then, and looked the part of mourner and penitent to admiration – being seedy and sick. He drank a great deal of brandy and water that night, and called in Farmer Dobbs, for want of better company, to drink with him; and told him all his grievances, and how happy he and 'the poor lady upstairs' might have been, had it not been for liars, and pick-thanks, and tale-bearers, and the like, who came between them – meaning Molly Doyle – whom, as he waxed eloquent over his liquor, he came at last to curse and rail at by name, with more than his accustomed freedom. And he described his own natural character and amiability in such moving terms, that he wept maudlin tears of sensibility over his theme; and when Dobbs was gone, drank some more grog, and took to railing and cursing again by himself, and then mounted the stairs unsteadily, to see 'what the Devil Doyle and the other – – – old witches were about in poor Peg's room'.

When he pushed open the door, he found some half-dozen crones, chiefly Irish, from the neighbouring town of Hackleton, sitting over the tea and snuff, etcetera, with candles lighted round the corpse, which was arrayed in a strangely cut robe of brown serge. She had secretly belonged to some order – I think the Carmelites, but I am not certain – and wore the habit in her coffin.

'What the devil are you doing with my wife?' asked the Captain, rather thickly. 'How dare you dress her up in this – – – trumpery, you – you cheating old witch; and what's that candle doing in her hand?'

I think he was a little startled, for the spectacle was grisly enough. The dead lady was arrayed in this strange brown robe, and in her rigid fingers, as in a socket, with the large wooden beads and cross wound around it, burned a wax candle, shedding its white light over the sharp features of the corpse. Moll Doyle was not to be put down by the Captain, whom she hated, and accordingly, in her phrase, 'he got as good as he gave'. And the Captain's wrath waxed fiercer, and he chucked the wax taper from the dead hand, and was on the point of flinging it at the silly old serving-woman's head.

'The holy candle, you sinner!' cried she.

'I've a good mind to make you eat it, you beast,' cried the Captain.

But I think he had not known before what it was, for he subsided a little sulkily, and he stuffed his hand with the candle (quite extinct by this time) into his pocket, and said he:

'You know devilish well you had no business going on with y-y-your damned *witch*-craft about my poor wife, without my leave – you do – and you'll please to take off that damned brown pinafore, and get her decently into her coffin, and I'll pitch your devil's wax light into the sink.'

And the Captain stalked out of the room.

'An' now her poor sowl's in prison, you wretch, be the mains o' ye; an' may yer own be shut into the wick o' that same candle, till it's burned out, ye savage.'

'I'd have you ducked for a witch, for two-pence,' roared the Captain up the staircase, with his hand on the banister, standing in the lobby. But the door of the chamber of death clapped angrily, and he went down to the parlour, where he examined the holy candle for a while, with a tipsy gravity, and then with something of that reverential feel for the symbolic, which is not uncommon in rakes and scamps, he thoughtfully locked it up in a press, where he ac-cumulated all sorts of obsolete rubbish-soiled packs of cards, disused tobacco-pipes, broken powder-flasks, his military sword, and a dusky bundle of the 'Flash Songster', and other questionable literature.

He did not trouble the dead lady's room any more. Being a voluble man it is probable that more cheerful plans and occupations began to entertain his fancy.

3.

So the poor lady was buried decently, and Captain Walshawe reigned alone for many years at Wauling. He was too shrewd and too experienced by this time to run violently down the steep hill that leads to ruin. So there was a method in his madness; and after a widowed career of more than forty years, he, too, died at least with some guineas in his purse.

Forty years and upwards is a great *edax rerum,* and a wonderful chemical power. It acted forcibly upon the gay Captain Walshawe. Gout supervened, and was no more conducive to temper than to enjoyment, and made his elegant hands lumpy at the small joints, and turned them slowly into crippled claws. He grew stout when his exercise was interfered with, and ultimately almost corpulent. He suffered from what Mr Hollyway calls 'bad legs', and was wheeled about in a great leathern-backed chair, and his infirmities went on accumulating with his years.

I am sorry to say, I never heard that he repented, or turned his thoughts seriously to the future. On the contrary, his talk grew fouler, and his fun ran upon his favourite sins, and his temper waxed more truculent. But he did not sink into dotage. Considering his bodily infirmities, his energies and his malignities, which were many and active, were marvellously little abated by time. So he went on to the close. When his temper was stirred, he cursed and swore in a way that made decent people tremble. It was a word and a blow with him; the latter, luckily, not very sure now. But he would seize his crutch and make a swoop or a pound at the offender, or shy his medicine-bottle, or his tumbler, at his head.

It was a peculiarity of Captain Walshawe, that he, by this time, hated nearly everybody. My uncle, Mr Watson, of Huddlestone, was cousin to the captain, and his heir-at-law. But my uncle had lent him money on mortgage of his estates, and there had been a treaty to sell, and terms and a price were agreed upon, in 'articles' which the lawyers said were still in force.

I think the ill-conditioned captain bore him a grudge of being richer than he, and would have liked to do him an ill turn. But it did not lie in his way; at least while he was living.

My Uncle Watson was a Methodist, and what they call a 'class-leader', and, on the whole, a very good man. He was now near fifty – grave, as beseemed his profession – somewhat dry – and a little severe, perhaps – but a just man.

A letter from the Penlynden doctor reached him at Huddlestone, announcing the death of the wicked old Captain; and suggesting his attendance at the funeral, and the expediency of his being on the spot to look after things at Wauling. The reasonableness of this striking my good uncle, he made his journey to the old house in Lancashire incontinently, and reached it in time for the funeral.

My uncle, whose traditions of the Captain were derived from his mother, who remembered him in his slim, handsome youth – in shorts, cocked-hat and lace, was amazed at the bulk of the coffin which contained his mortal remains; but the lid being screwed down, he did not see the face of the bloated old sinner.

4.

What I relate, I had from the lips of my uncle, who was a truthful man, and not prone to fancies.

The day turning out awfully rainy and tempestuous, he persuaded the doctor and the attorney to remain for the night at Wauling.

There was no will – the attorney was sure of that; for the Captain's enmities were perpetually shifting, and he could never quite make up his mind, as to how best to give effect to a malignity whose direction was being constantly modified. He had had instructions for drawing a will a dozen times over. But the process had always been arrested by the intending testator.

Search being made, no will was found. The papers, indeed, were all right, with one important exception: the leases were nowhere to be seen. There were special circumstances connected with several of the principal tenancies on the estate – unnecessary here to detail – which rendered the loss of the documents one of very serious moment, and even of very obvious danger.

My uncle, therefore, searched strenuously. The attorney was at his elbow, and the doctor helped with a suggestion now and then. The old serving-man seemed an honest deaf creature, and really knew nothing.

My Uncle Watson was very much perturbed. He fancied – but this possibly was only fancy – that he had detected for a moment a queer look in the attorney's face; and from that instant it became fixed in his mind that he knew all about the leases. Mr Watson expounded that evening in the parlour to the doctor, the attorney and the deaf servant. Ananias and Sapphira figured in the foreground; and the awful

'... clusters of worms into wriggling knots of sparks ... were drawn
into the fireplace and up the rapacious old chimney ...' (see p. 127)

nature of fraud and theft, or tampering in any wise with the plain rule of honesty in matters pertaining to estates, etcetera, were pointedly dwelt upon; and then came a long and strenuous prayer, in which he entreated with fervour and aplomb that the hard heart of the sinner who had abstracted the leases might be softened or broken in such a way as to lead to their restitution; or that, if he continued reserved and contumacious, it might at least be the will of Heaven to bring him to public justice and the documents to light. The fact is, that he was praying all this time at the attorney.

When these religious exercises were over, the visitors retired to their rooms, and my Uncle Watson wrote two or three pressing letters by the fire. When his task was done, it had grown late; the candles were flaring in their sockets, and all in bed, and, I suppose, asleep, but he.

The fire was nearly out, he chilly, and the flame of the candles throbbing strangely in their sockets shed alternate glare and shadow round the old wainscoted room and its quaint furniture. Outside were the wild thunder and piping of the storm; and the rattling of distant windows sounded through the passages, and down the stairs, like angry people astir in the house.

My Uncle Watson belongs to a sect who by no means reject the supernatural, and whose founder, on the contrary, has sanctioned ghosts in the most emphatic way. He was glad, therefore, to remember, that in prosecuting his search that day, he had seen some six inches of wax candle in the press in the parlour; for he had no fancy to be overtaken by darkness in his present situation. He had no time to lose; and taking the bunch of keys – of which he was no master – he soon fitted the lock and secured the candle – a treasure in the circumstances; and lighting it, he stuffed it into the socket of the expiring candles, and extinguishing the other, he looked round the room in the steady light reassured. At the same moment, an unusually violent gust of the storm blew a handful of gravel against the parlour window, with a sharp rattle that startled him in the midst of the roar and hubbub; and the flame of the candle itself was agitated by the air.

5.

My uncle walked up to bed, guarding his candle with his hand, for the lobby windows were rattling furiously, and he disliked the idea of being left in the dark more than ever.

The bedroom was comfortable, though old-fashioned. He shut and bolted the door. There was a tall looking-glass opposite the foot of the four-poster, on the dressing-table between the windows. He tried to make the curtains meet, but they would not draw, and like many a gentleman in a like perplexity, he did not possess a pin, nor was there one in the huge pin cushion beneath the glass.

He turned the face of the mirror away therefore, so that its back was presented to the bed, pulled the curtains together, and placed a chair against them, to prevent their falling open again. There was a good fire, and a reinforcement of round coal and wood inside the fender. So he piled it up to ensure a cheerful blaze through the night, and placing a little black mahogany table, with the legs of a Satyr, beside the bed, and his candle upon it, he got between the sheets, and laid his red-capped head upon his pillow, and disposed himself to sleep.

The first thing that made him uncomfortable was a sound at the foot of his bed, quite distinct in a momentary lull of the storm. It was only the gentle rustle and rush of the curtains, which fell open again; and as his eyes opened, he saw them resuming their perpendicular dependence, and sat up in his bed almost expecting to see something uncanny in the aperture.

There was nothing, however, but the dressing-table, and other dark furniture, and the window-curtains faintly undulating in the violence of the storm. He did not care to get up therefore – the fire being bright and cheery – to replace the curtains by a chair, in the position in which he had left them, anticipating possibly a new recurrence of the relapse which had startled him from his incipient doze.

So he got to sleep in a little while again, but he was disturbed by a sound, as he fancied, at the table on which stood the candle. He could not say what it was, only that he wakened with a start, and lying so in some amaze, he did distinctly hear a sound which startled him a good deal, though there was nothing necessarily supernatural in it. He described it as resembling what would occur if you fancied a thin-nish table-leaf, with a convex warp in it, depressed the reverse way, and suddenly with a spring recovering its natural convexity. It was a loud, sudden thump, which made the heavy candlestick jump, and there was an end, except that my uncle did not get again into a doze for ten minutes at least.

The next time he awoke, it was in that odd, serene way that sometimes occurs. We open our eyes, we know not why, quite placidly, and are on the instant wide awake. He had a nap of some duration this time, for his candle-flame was fluttering and flaring, *in articulo,* in the silver socket. But the fire was still bright and cheery; so he popped the extinguisher on the socket, and almost at the same time there came a tap at his door, and a sort of crescendo 'hush-sh-sh!' Once more my Uncle was sitting up, scared and perturbed in his bed. He recollected, however, that he had bolted his door; and such inveterate materialists are we in the midst of our spiritualism, that this reassured him, and he breathed a deep sigh, and began to grow tranquil. But after a rest of a minute or two, there came a louder and sharper knock at his door; so that instinctively he called out, 'Who's there?' in a loud, stern key. There was no sort of response, however. The nervous effect of the start subsided; and I think my uncle must have remembered how constantly, especially on a stormy night, these creaks or cracks which simulate all manner of goblin noises, make themselves naturally audible.

6.

After a while, then, he lay down with his back turned towards that side of the bed at which was the door, and his face toward the table on which stood the massive old candlestick, capped with its extinguisher, and in that position he closed his eyes. But sleep would not revisit them. All kinds of queer fancies began to trouble him – some of them I remember.

He felt the point of a finger, he averred, pressed most distinctly on the top of his great toe, as if a living hand were between his sheets, and making a sort of signal of attention or silence. Then again he felt something bounce in the middle of his bolster, just under his head. Then a voice said, 'Oh!' very gently, close at the back of his head. All these things he felt certain of, and yet investigation led to nothing. He felt odd little cramps stealing now and then about him, and then, on a sudden, the middle finger of his right hand was plucked backwards, with a light playful jerk that frightened him awfully.

Meanwhile the storm kept singing and howling, and ha-ha-hooing hoarsely among the limbs of the old trees and the chimney-pots; and my Uncle Watson, although he prayed and meditated as was his wont when he lay awake, felt his heart throb excitedly, and sometimes thought he was beset with evil spirits, and at others that he was in the early stages of a fever.

He resolutely kept his eyes closed, however, and, like St Paul's shipwrecked companions, wished for the day. At last another little doze seems to have stolen upon his senses, for he awoke quietly and completely as before – opening his eyes all at once, and seeing everything as if he had not slept for a moment.

The fire was still blazing redly – nothing uncertain in the light – the massive silver candlestick, topped with its tall extinguisher, stood in the centre of the black mahogany table as before; and, looking by what seemed a sort of accident to the apex of this, he beheld something which made him quite misdoubt the evidence of his eyes.

He saw the extinguisher lifted by a tiny hand, from beneath, and a small human face, no bigger than a thumbnail, with nicely proportioned features peep from beneath it. In this Lilliputian countenance was such a ghastly consternation as horrified my uncle unspeakably. Out came a little foot then and there, and a pair of wee legs, in short silk stockings and buckled shoes, then the rest of the figure; and, with the arms holding about the socket, the little legs stretched and stretched, hanging about the stem of the candlestick till the feet reached the base, and so down the Satyr-like leg of the table, till they reached the floor, extending elastically, and strangely enlarging in all proportions as they approached the ground, where the feet and buckles were those of a well-shaped, fully grown man, and the figure tapering upward until it dwindled to its original fairy dimensions at the top, like an object seen in some strangely curved mirror.

Standing upon the floor he expanded, my amazed uncle could not tell how, into his proper proportions; and stood pretty nearly in profile at the bedside, a handsome and elegantly shaped young man, in a bygone military costume, with a small laced, three-cocked hat and plume on his head, but looking like a man going to be hanged – in unspeakable despair.

He stepped lightly to the hearth, and turned for a few seconds, very dejectedly with his back toward the bed and the mantel-piece, and he saw the hilt of his rapier glittering in the firelight; and then walking across the room he placed himself at the dressing-table, visible through the divided curtains at the foot of the bed. The fire was blazing still so brightly that my uncle saw him as distinctly as if half a dozen candles were burning.

7.

The looking-glass was an old-fashioned piece of furniture, and had a drawer beneath it. My uncle had searched it carefully for the papers in the day time; but the silent figure pulled the drawer quite out, pressed a spring at the side, disclosing a false receptacle behind it, and from this he drew a parcel of papers tied together with pink tape.

All this time my uncle was staring at him in a horrified state, neither winking nor breathing and the apparation had not once given the smallest intimation of consciousness that a living person was in the same room. But now, for the first time, it turned its livid stare full upon my uncle with a hateful smile of significance, lifting up the little parcel of papers between his slender finger and thumb. Then he made a long, cunning wink at him, and seemed to blow out one of his cheeks in a burlesque grimace which, but for the horrific circumstances, would have been ludicrous. My uncle could not tell whether this was really an intentional distortion or only one of those horrid ripples and deflections which were constantly disturbing the proportions of the figure, as if it were seen through some unequal and perverting medium.

The figure now approached the bed, seeming to grow exhausted and malignant as it did so. My uncle's terror nearly culminated at this point, for he believed it was drawing near to him with an evil purpose. But it was not so; for the soldier, over whom twenty years seemed to have passed in his brief transit to the dressing-table and back again, threw himself into a great high-backed arm-chair of stuffed leather at the far side of the fire, and placed his heels on the fender. His feet and legs seemed instinctively to swell, and swathings showed themselves round them, and they grew into something enormous, and the upper figure swayed and shaped itself into corresponding proportions, a great mass of corpulence, with a cadaverous and malignant face, and the furrows of a great old age, and colourless glassy eyes; and with these changes, which came indefinitely but rapidly as those of a sunset cloud, the fine regimentals faded away, and a loose, gray, woollen drapery, somehow, was there in its stead; and all seemed to be stained and rotten, for swarms of worms seemed creeping in and out, while the figure grew paler and paler, till my uncle, who liked his pipe, and employed the simile naturally, said the whole effigy grew to the colour of tobacco ashes, and the clusters of worms into little wriggling knots of sparks such as we see running over the residuum of a burnt sheet of paper. And so with the strong draught caused by the fire, and the current of air from the window, which was rattling in the storm, the feet seemed to be drawn into the fire-place, and the whole figure, light as ashes, floated away with them, and disappeared with a whisk up the rapacious old chimney.

It seemed to my uncle that the fire suddenly darkened and the air grew icy cold, and there came an awful roar and riot of tempest, which shook the old house from top to base, and sounded like the yelling of a blood-thirsty mob on receiving a new and long-expected victim.

Good Uncle Watson used to say, 'I have been in many situations of fear and danger in the course of my life, but never did I pray with so much agony before or since; for then, as now, it was clear beyond a cavil that I had actually beheld the phantom of an evil spirit.'

8.

Now there are two curious circumstances to be observed in this relation of my uncle's, who was, as I have said, a perfectly veracious man.

First – The wax candle which he took from the press in the parlour and burnt at his bedside on that horrible night was unquestionably, according to the testimony of the old deaf servant, who had been fifty years at Wauling, the identical piece of 'holy candle' which had stood in the fingers of the poor lady's corpse, and concerning which the old Irish crone, long since dead, had delivered the curious curse I have mentioned against the Captain.

Secondly – Behind the drawer under the looking-glass, he did actually discover a second but secret drawer, in which were concealed the identical papers which he had suspected the attorney of having made

128

away with. There were circumstances, too, afterwards disclosed which convinced my uncle that the old man had deposited them there preparatory to burying them, which he had nearly made up his mind to do.

Now, a very remarkable ingredient in this tale of my Uncle Watson was this, that so far as my father, who had never seen Captain Walshawe in the course of his life, could gather, the phantom had exhibited a horrible and grotesque, but unmistakeable resemblance to that defunct scamp in the various stages of his long life.

Wauling was sold in the year 1837, and the old house shortly after pulled down, and a new one built nearer to the river. I often wonder whether it was rumoured to be haunted, and, if so, what stories were current about it. It was a commodious and staunch old house, and withal rather handsome; and its demolition was certainly suspicious.

6

Madam Crowl's Ghost

I'M AN OLD woman now, and I was but thirteen my last birthday, the night I came to Applewale House. My aunt was the housekeeper there, and a sort o' one-horse carriage was down at Lexhoe to take me and my box up to Applewale.

I was a bit frightened by the time I got to Lexhoe, and when I saw the carriage and horse, I wished myself back again with my mother at Hazleden. I was crying when I got into the 'shay' – that's what we used to call it – and old John Mulbery that drove it, and was a good-natured fellow, bought me a handful of apples at the Golden Lion to cheer me up a bit; and he told me that there was a currant-cake, and tea, and pork-chops, waiting for me, all hot, in my aunt's room at the great house. It was a fine moonlight night and I ate the apples, lookin' out o' the shay winda.

It's a shame for gentlemen to frighten a poor child like I was. I sometimes think it might be tricks. There was two on 'em on the tap o' the coach beside me. And they began to question me after nightfall, when the moon rose, where I was going to. Well, I told them it was to wait on Dame Arabella Crowl, of Applewale House, near by Lexhoe.

'Ho, then,' says one of them, 'you'll not be long there!'

And I looked at him as much as to say 'Why not?' for I had spoken out when I told them where I was goin', as it 'twas some thing clever I had to say.

'Because,' says he, 'and don't you for your life tell no one, only watch her and see – she's possessed by the devil, and more an half a ghost. Have you got a Bible?'

132

'Yes, sir,' says I. For my mother put my little Bible in my box, and I knew it was there: and by the same token, though the print's too small for my ald eyes, I have it in my press to this hour.

As I looked up at him saying 'Yes sir,' I thought I saw him winkin' at his friend; but I could not be sure.

'Well,' says he, 'be sure you put it under your bolster every night, it will keep the ald girl's claws aff ye.'

And I got such a fright when he said that, you wouldn't fancy! And I'd a liked to ask him a lot about the ald lady, but I was too shy, and he and his friend began talkin' together about their own consarns, and dowly enough I got down, as I told ye, at Lexhoe. My heart sank as I drove into the dark avenue. The trees stand very thick and big, as ald as the ald house almost, and four people, with their arms out and finger-tips touchin', barely girds round some of them.

Well, my neck was stretched out o' the winda, looking for the first view o' the great house; and all at once we pulled up in front of it.

A great white-and-black house it is, wi' great black beams across and right up it, and gables lookin' out, as white as a sheet, to the moon, and the shadows o' the trees, two or three up and down in front, you could count the leaves on them and all the little diamond-shaped winda-panes, glimmering on the great hall winda, and great shutters, in the old fashion, hinged on the wall outside, boulted across all the rest o' the windas in front, for there was but three or four servants, and the old lady in the house, and most o' t'rooms was locked up.

My heart was in my mouth when I sid the journey was over, and this, the great house afoore me, and I sa near my aunt that I never sid till noo, and Dame Crowl, that I was come to wait upon, and was afeard on already.

My aunt kissed me in the hall, and brought me to her room. She was tall and thin, wi' a pale face and black eyes, and long thin hands wi' black mittins on. She was past fifty, and her word was short; but her word was law. I hev no complaints to make of her; but she was a hard woman, and I think she would hev bin kinder to me if I had bin her sister's child in place of her brother's. But all that's o' no consequence noo.

The squire – his name was Mr. Chevenix Crowl, he was Dame Crowl's grandson – came down there, by way of seeing that the old lady was well treated, about twice of thrice in the year. I sid him but twice all the time I was at Applewale House.

I can't say but she was well taken care of, notwithstandin'; but that was because my aunt and Meg Wyvern, that was her maid, had a conscience, and did their duty by her.

Mrs Wyvern – Meg Wyvern my aunt called her to herself, and Mrs Wyvern to me – was a fat, jolly lass of fifty, a good height and a good breadth, always good-humoured and walked slow. She had fine wages, but she was a bit stingy, and kept all her fine clothes under lock and key, and wore, mostly, a twilled chocolate cotton, wi' red, and yellow, and green sprigs and balls on it, and it lasted wonderful.

She never gave me nout, not the vally o' a brass thimble, all the time I was there; but she was good-humoured, and always laughin', and she talked no end o' proas over her tea; and, seeing me sa sackless and dowly, she roused me up wi' her laughin' and stories; and I think I liked her better than my aunt – children is so taken wi' a bit o' fun or a story – though my aunt was very good to me, but a hard woman about some things, and silent always.

My aunt took me into her bed-chamber, that I might rest myself a bit while she was settin' the tea in her room. But first, she patted me on the shoulder, and said I was a tall lass o' my years, and had spired up well, and asked me if I could do plain work and stitchin'; and she looked in my face, and said I was like my father, her brother, that was dead and gone, and she hoped I was a better Christian, and wad na du a' that lids.

It was a hard sayin' the first time I set foot in her room, I thought.

When I went into the next room, the housekeeper's room – very comfortable, yak (oak) all round – there was a fine fire blazin' away, wi' coal, and peat, and wood, all in a low together, and tea on the table, and hot cake, and smokin' meat; and there was Mrs Wyvern, fat, jolly, and talkin' away, more in an hour than my aunt would in a year.

While I was still at my tea my aunt went up-stairs to see Madam Crowl.

'She's agone up to see that old Judith Squailes is awake,' says Mrs Wyvern. 'Judith sits with Madam

Crowl when me and Mrs Shutters' – that was my aunt's name – 'is away. She's a troublesome old lady. Ye'll hev to be sharp wi' her, or she'll be into the fire, or out o' t' winda. She goes on wires, she does, old though she be.'

'How old, ma'am?' says I.

'Ninety-three her last birthday, and that's eight months gone,' says she; and she laughed. 'And don't be askin' questions about her before your aunt – mind, I tell ye; just take her as you find her, and that's all.'

'And what's to be my business about her, please, ma'am?' says I.

'About the old lady? Well,' says she, 'your aunt, Mrs Shutters, will tell you that; but I suppose you'll hev to sit in the room with your work, and see she's at no mischief, and let her amuse herself with her things on the table, and get her her food or drink as she calls for it, and keep her out o' mischief, and ring the bell hard if she's troublesome.'

'Is she deaf, ma'am?'

'No, nor blind,' says she; 'as sharp as a needle, but she's gone quite aupy, and can't remember nout rightly; and Jack the Giant Killer, or Goody Twoshoes will please her as well as the king's court, or the affairs of the nation.'

'And what did the little girl go away for, ma'am, that went on Friday last? My aunt wrote to my mother she was to go.'

'Yes; she's gone.'

'What for?' says I again.

'She didn't answer Mrs Shutters, I do suppose,' says

136

she. 'I don't know. Don't be talkin'; your aunt can't abide a talkin' child.'

'And please, ma'am, is the old lady well in health?' says I.

'It ain't no harm to ask that,' says she. 'She's torflin' a bit lately, but better this week past, and I dare say she'll last out her hundred years yet. Hish! Here's your aunt coming down the passage.'

In comes my aunt, and begins talkin' to Mrs Wyvern, and I, beginnin' to feel more comfortable and at home like, was walkin' about the room lookin' at this thing and at that. There was pretty old china things on the cupboard, and pictures again the wall; and there was a door open in the wainscot, and I sees a queer old leathern jacket, wi' straps and buckles to it, and sleeves as long as the bed-post hangin' up inside.

'What's that you're at, child?' says my aunt, sharp enough, turning about when I thought she least minded. 'What's that in your hand?'

'This ma'am?' says I, turning about with the leathern jacket. 'I don't know what it is, ma'am.'

Pale as she was, the red came up in her cheeks, and her eyes flashed wi' anger, and I think only she had half a dozen steps to take, between her and me, she'd a gev me a sizzup. But she did gie me a shake by the shouther, and she plucked the thing out o' my hand, and says she, 'While ever you stay here, don't ye meddle wi' nout that don't belong to ye,' and she hung it up on the pin that was there, and shut the door wi' a bang and locked it fast.

Mrs Wyvern was liftin' up her hands and laughin'

all this time, quietly, in her chair, rolling herself a bit in it, as she used when she was kinkin'.

The tears was in my eyes, and she winked at my aunt, and says she, dryin' her own eyes that was wet wi' the laughin', 'Tut, the child meant no harm – come here to me, child. It's only a pair o' crutches for lame ducks, and ask us no questions mind, and we'll tell ye no lies; and come here and sit down, and drink a mug o' beer before ye go to your bed.'

My room, mind ye, was upstairs, next to the old lady's, and Mrs Wyvern's bed was near hers in her room, and I was to be ready at call, if need should be.

The old lady was in one of her tantrums that night and part of the day before. She used to take fits o' the sulks. Sometimes she would not let them dress her, and at other times she would not let them take her clothes off. She was a great beauty, they said, in her day. But there was no one about Applewale that remembered her in her prime. And she was dreadful fond o' dress, and had thick silks, and stiff satins, and velvets, and laces, and all sorts, enough to set up seven shops at the least. All her dresses was old-fashioned and queer, but worth a fortune.

Well, I went to my bed. I lay for a while awake; for a' things was new to me; and I think the tea was in my nerves, too, for I wasn't used to it, except now and then on a holiday or the like. And I heard Mrs Wyvern talkin', and I listened with my hand to my ear; but I could not hear Mrs Crowl, and I don't think she said a word.

There was great care took of her. The people at Applewale knew that when she died they would every one get the sack; and their situations was well paid and easy.

The doctor came twice a week to see the old lady, and you may be sure they all did as he bid them. One thing was the same every time; they were never to cross or frump her, any way, but to humour and please her in everything.

So she lay in her clothes all that night, and next day, not a word she said, and I was at my needlework all that day, in my own room, except when I went down to my dinner.

I would a liked to see the ald lady, and even to hear her speak. But she might as well a' bin in Lunnon a' the time for me.

When I had my dinner my aunt sent me out for a walk for an hour. I was glad when I came back, the trees was so big, and the place so dark and lonesome, and 'twas a cloudy day, and I cried a deal, thinkin' of home, while I was walkin' alone there. That evening, the candles bein' alight, I was sittin' in my room, and the door was open into Madam Crowl's chamber, where my aunt was. It was, then, for the first time I heard what I suppose was the ald lady talking.

It was a queer noise like, I couldn't well say which, a bird, or a beast, only it had a bleatin' sound in it, and was very small.

I pricked my ears to hear all I could. But I could not make out one word she said. And my aunt answered:

'The evil one can't hurt no one, ma'am, bout the Lord permits.'

Then the same queer voice from the bed says

something more that I couldn't make head nor tail
on.

And my aunt med answer again: 'Let them pull
faces, ma'am, and say what they will; if the Lord be
for us, who can be against us?'

I kept listenin' with my ear turned to the door,
holdin' my breath, but not another word or sound
came in from the room. In about twenty minutes, as
I was sittin' by the table, lookin' at the picture in the
old Aesop's Fables, I was aware o' something moving
at the door, and lookin' up I sid my aunt's face
lookin' in at the door, and her hand raised.

'Hish!' says she, very soft, and comes over to me on
tiptoe, and she says in a whisper: 'Thank God, she's
asleep at last, and don't ye make no noise till I come
back, for I'm goin' down to take my cup o' tea, and
I'll be back i' noo – me and Mrs Wyvern, and she'll
be sleepin' in the room, and you can run down when
we come up, and Judith will gie ye yaur supper in my
room.'

And with that she goes.

I kep' looking at the picture-book, as before, listenin' every noo and then, but there was no sound,
not a breath, that I could hear; an' I began whisperin'
to the pictures and talkin' to myself to keep my heart
up, for I was growin' feared in that big room.

And at last up I got, and began walkin' about the
room, lookin' at this and peepin' at that, to amuse my
mind, ye'll understand. And at last what sud I do but
peeps into Madam Crowl's bedchamber.

A grand chamber it was, wi' a great four-poster,
wi' flowered silk curtains as tall as the ceilin', and

'... The big looking glass, that the old lady used to look into and admire herself...'

(see p. 147)

foldin' down on the floor, and drawn close all round. There was a lookin'-glass, the biggest I ever sid before, and the room was a blaze o' light. I counted twenty-two wax candles, all alight. Such was her fancy, and no one dared say her nay.

I listened at the door, and gaped and wondered all round. When I heard there was not a breath, and did not see so much as a stir in the curtains, I took heart, and walked into the room on tiptoe, and looked round again. Then I takes a keek at myself in the big glass; and at last it came in my head, 'Why couldn't I ha' a keek at the ald lady herself in the bed?'

Ye'd think me a fule if ye knew half how I longed to see Dame Crowl, and I thought to myself if I didn't peep now I might wait many a day before I got so gude a chance again.

Well, my dear, I came to the side o' the bed, the curtains bein' close, and my heart a'most failed me. But I took courage, and I slips my finger in between the thick curtains, and then my hand. So I waits a bit, but all was still as death. So softly, softly I draws the curtain, and there, sure enough, I sid before me, stretched out like the painted lady on the tomb-stean in Lexhoe Church, the famous Dame Crowl, of Applewale House.

There she was, dressed out. You never sid the like in they days. Satin and silk, and scarlet and green, and gold and pint lace; by Jen! 'twas a sight! A big powdered wig, half as high as herself, was a-top o' her head, and wow! – was ever such wrinkles? – and her old baggy throat all powdered white, and her cheeks rouged, and mouse-skin eyebrows, that Mrs

Wyvern used to stick on, and there she lay proud and stark, wi' a pair o' clocked silk hose on, and heels to her shoon as tall as nine-pins. Lawk! But her nose was crooked and thin, and half the whites o' her eyes was open. She used to stand, dressed as she was, gigglin' and dribblin' before the lookin'-glass wi' a fan in her hand and a big nosegay in her bodice. Her wrinkled little hands was stretched down by her sides, and such long nails, all cut into points, I never sid in my days. Could it even a bin the fashion for grit fowk to wear their fingernails so?

Well, I think ye'd a-bin frightened yourself if ye'd a sid such a sight. I couldn't let go the curtain, nor move an inch, nor take my eyes off her; my very heart stood still. And in an instant she opens her eyes and up she sits, and spins herself round, and down wi' her, wi' a clack on her two tall heels on the floor, facin' me, ogglin' in my face wi' her two great glassy eyes, and a wicked simper wi' her wrinkled lips, and lang fause teeth.

Well, a corpse is a natural thing; but this was the dreadfullest sight I ever sid. She had her fingers straight out pointin' at me, and her back was crooked, round again wi' age. Says she:

'Ye little limb! what for did ye say I killed the boy? I'll tickle ye till ye're stiff!'

If I'd a thought an instant, I'd a turned about and run. But I couldn't take my eyes off her, and I backed from her as soon as I could; and she came clatterin' after like a thing on wires, with her fingers pointing to my throat, and she makin' all the time a sound with her tongue like zizz-zizz-zizz.

I kept backin' and backin' as quick as I could, and her fingers was only a few inches away from my throat, and I felt I'd lose my wits if she touched me.

I went back this way, right into the corner, and I gev a yellock, ye'd think saul and body was partin', and that minute my aunt, from the door, calls out wi' a blare, and the ald lady turns round on her, and I turns about, and ran through my room, and down the stairs, as hard as my legs could carry me.

I cried hearty, I can tell you, when I got down to the housekeeper's room. Mrs Wyvern laughed a deal when I told her what happened. But she changed her key when she heard the ald lady's words.

'Say them again,' says she.

So I told her.

'Ye little limb! What for did ye say I killed the boy? I'll tickle ye till ye're stiff.'

'And did ye say she killed a boy?' says she.

'Not I, ma'am,' says I.

Judith was always up with me, after that, when the two elder women was away from her. I would a jumped out at winda, rather than stay alone in the same room wi' her.

It was about a week after, as well as I can remember, Mrs Wyvern, one day when me and her was alone, told me a thing about Madam Crowl that I did not know before.

She being young and a great beauty, full seventy year before, had married Squire Crowl, of Applewale. But he was a widower, and had a son about nine years old.

There never was tale or tidings of this boy after

144

one mornin'. No one could say where he went to. He was allowed too much liberty, and used to be off in the morning, one day, to the keeper's cottage and breakfast wi' him, and away to the warren, and not home, mayhap, till evening; and another time down to the lake, and bathe there, and spend the day fishin' there, or paddlin' about in the boat. Well, no one could say what was gone wi' him; only this, that his hat was found by the lake, under a haathorn that grows thar to this day, and 'twas thought he was drowned bathin'. And the squire's son, by his second marriage, by this Madam Crowl that lived sa dreadful lang, came in far the estates. It was his son, the ald lady's grandson, Squire Chevenix Crowl, the owned the estates at the time I came to Applewale.

There was a deal o' talk lang before my aunt's time about it; and 'twas said the step-mother knew more than she was like to let out. And she managed her husband, the ald squire, wi' her white-heft and flatteries. And as the boy was never seen more, in course of time the thing died out of fowks' minds.

I'm goin' to tell ye noo about what I sid wi' my own een.

I was not there six months, and it was winter time, when the ald lady took her last sickness.

The doctor was afeard she might a took a fit o' madness, as she did fifteen years befoore, and was buckled up, many a time, in a strait-waistcoat, which was the very leathern jerkin I sid in the closet, off my aunt's room.

Well, she didn't. She pined, and windered, and went off, torflin', torflin', quiet enough, till a day or two before her flittin', and then she took to rabblin', and sometimes skirlin' in the bed, ye'd think a robber had a knife to her throat, and she used to work out o' the bed, and not being strong enough, then, to walk or stand, she'd fall on the flure, wi' her ald wizened hands stretched before her face, and skirlin' still for mercy.

Ye may guess I didn't go into the room, and I used to be shiverin' in my bed wi' fear, at her skirlin' and scrafflin' on the flure, and blarin' out words that id make your skin turn blue.

My aunt, and Mrs Wyvern, and Judith Squailes, and a woman from Lexhoe, was always about her. At last she took fits, and they wore her out.

T' sir (parson) was there, and prayed for her; but she was past praying with. I suppose it was right, but none could think there was much good in it, and sa at lang last she made her flittin', and a' was over, and old Dame Crowl was shrouded and coffined, and Squire Chevenix was wrote for. But he was away in France, and the delay was sa lang, that t' sir and doctor both agreed it would not du to keep her langer out o' her place, and no one cared but just them two, and my aunt and the rest o' us, from Applewale, to go to the buryin'. So the old lady of Applewale was laid in the vault under Lexhoe Church; and we lived up at the great house till such time as the squire should come to tell his will about us, and pay off such as he chose to discharge.

I was put into another room, two doors away from what was Dame Crowl's chamber, after her death, and this thing happened the night before Squire Chevenix came to Applewale.

The room I was in now was a large square chamber, covered wi' yak pannels, but unfurnished except for my bed, which had no curtains to it, and a chair and a table, or so, that looked nothing at all in such a big room. And the big looking-glass, that the old lady used to keek into and admire herself from head to heel, now that there was na mair o' that wark, was put out of the way, and stood against the wall in my room, for there was shiftin' o' many things in her chamber ye may suppose, when she came to be coffined.

The news had come that day that the squire was to be down next morning at Applewale; and not sorry was I, for I thought I was sure to be sent home again to my mother. And right glad was I, and I was thinkin' of a' at hame, and my sister Janet, and the kitten and the pymag, and Trimmer the tike, and all the rest, and I got sa fidgetty, I couldn't sleep, and the clock struck twelve, and me wide awake, and the room as dark as pick. My back was turned to the door, and my eyes toward the wall opposite.

Well, it could na be a full quarter past twelve, when I sees a lightin' on the wall befoore me, as if something took fire behind, and the shadas o' the bed, and the chair, and my gown, that was hangin' from the wall, was dancin' up and down on the ceilin' beams and the yak pannels; and I turns my head ower my shouther quick, thinkin' something must a gone a' fire.

And what sud I see, by Jen! but the likeness o' the

ald beldame, bedizened out in her satins and velvets, on her dead body, simperin', wi' her eyes as wide as saucers, and her face like the fiend himself. 'Twas a red light that rose about her in a fuffin low, as if her dress round her feet was blazin'. She was drivin' on right for me, wi' her ald shrivelled hands crooked as if she was goin' to claw me. I could not stir, but she passed me straight by, wi' a blast o' cald air, and I sid her, at the wall, in the alcove as my aunt used to call it, which was a recess where the state bed used to stand in ald times wi' a door open wide, and her hands gropin' in at somethin' was there. I never sid that door befoore. And she turned round to me, like a thing on a pivot, flyrin', and all at once the room was dark, and I standin' at the far side o' the bed; I don't know how I got there, and I found my tongue at last, and if I did na blare a yellock, rennin' down the gallery and almost pulled Mrs Wyvern's door off t' hooks, and frightened her half out o' wits.

Ye may guess I did na sleep that night; and wi' the first light, down wi' me to my aunt, as fast as my two legs cud carry me.

Well my aunt did na frump of flite me, as I thought she would, but she held me by the hand, and looked hard in my face all the time. And she telt me not to be feared; and says she:

'Hed the appearance a key in its hand?'

'Yes,' says I, bringin' it to mind, 'a big key in a queer brass handle.'

'Stop a bit,' says she, lettin' go ma hand, and openin' the cupboard-door. 'Was it like this?' says she, takin' one out in her fingers, and showing it to me, with a dark look in my face.

'That was it,' says I, quick enough.

'Are ye sure?' she says, turnin' it round.

'Sart,' says I, and I felt like I was gain' to faint when I sid it.

'Well, that will do, child,' says she, saftly thinkin', and she locked it up again.

'The squire himself will be here today, before twelve o'clock, and ye must tell him all about it,' says she, thinkin', 'and I suppose I'll be leavin' soon, and so the best thing for the present is, that ye should go home this afternoon, and I'll look out another place for you when I can.'

Fain was I, ye may guess, at that word.

My aunt packed up my things for me, and the three pounds that was due to me, to bring home, and Squire Crowl himself came down to Applewale that day, a handsome man, about thirty years ald. It was the second time I sid him. But this was the first time he spoke to me.

My aunt talked wi' him in the housekeeper's room, and I don't know what they said. I was a bit feared on the squire, he bein' a great gentleman down in Lexhoe, and I darn't go near till I was called. And says he, smilin':

'What's a' this ye a sen, child? it mun be a dream, for ye know there's na sic a thing as a bo or a freet in a' the world. But whatever it was, ma little maid, sit ye down and tell all about it from first to last.'

Well, so soon as I made an end, he thought a bit, and says he to my aunt:

149

'I mind the place well. In old Sir Olivur's time lame Wyndel told me there was a door in that recess, to the left, where the lassie dreamed she saw my grandmother open it. He was past eighty when he told me that, and I but a boy. It's twenty year sen. The plate and jewels used to be kept there, long ago, before the iron closet was made in the arras chamber, and he told me, the key had a brass handle, and this ye say was found in the bottom o' the kist where she kept her old fans. Now, would not it be a queer thing if we found some spoons or diamonds forgot there? Ye mun come up wi' us, lassie, and point to the very spot.'

Loth was I, and my heart in my mouth, and fast I held by my aunt's hand as I stept into that awsome room, and showed them both how she came and passed me by, and the spot where she stood, and where the door seemed to open.

There was an ald empty press against the wall then, and shoving it aside, sure enough there was the tracing of a door in the wainscot, and a keyhole stopped with wood, and planed across as smooth as the rest, and the joining of the door all stopped wi' putty the colour o' yak, and, but for the hinges that showed a bit when the press was shoved aside, ye would not consayt there was a door there at all.

'Ha!' says he, wi' a queer smile, 'this looks like it.'

It took some minutes wi' a small chisel and hammer to pick the bit o' wood out o' the keyhole. The key fitted, sure enough, and, wi' a strang twist and a lang skreak, the boult went back and he pulled the door open.

There was another door inside, stranger than the first, but the lacks was gone, and it opened easy. Inside was a narrow floor and walls and vault o' brick; we could not see what was in it, for 'twas dark as pick.

When my aunt had lighted the candle, the squire held it up and stept in.

My aunt stood on tiptoe tryin' to look over his shoulder, and I did ne see nout.

'Ha! ha!' says the squire, steppin' backward. 'What's that? Gi' ma the poker – quick!' says he to my aunt. And as she went to the hearth I peeps beside his arm, and I sid squat down in the far corner a monkey of a flayin' on the chest, or else the maist shrivelled up, wizzened ald wife that ever was sen on yearth.

'By Jen!' says my aunt, as putting the poker in his hand, she keeked by his shouther, and sid the ill-favoured thing, 'hae a care, sir, what ye're doin'. Back wi' ye, and shut to the door!'

But in place o' that he steps in saftly, wi' the poker pointed like a swoord, and he gies it a poke, and down it a' tumbles together, head and a', in a heap o' bayans and dust, little meyar an' a hatful.

'Twas the bayans o' a child; a' the rest went to dust at a touch. They said nout for a while, but he turns round the skull, as it lay on the floor.

Young as I was, I consayted I knew well enough what they was thinkin' on.

'A dead cat!' says he, pushin' back and blowin' out the can'le, and shuttin' to the door. 'We'll come back, you and me, Mrs Shutters, and look on the shelves

THE HOURS AFTER MIDNIGHT

by-and-by. I've other matters first to speak to ye about; and this little girl's goin' hame, ye say. She has her wages, and I mun mak' her a present,' says he, pattin' my shouther wi' his hand.

And he did gimma a goud pound and I went aff to Lexhoe about an hour after, and sa hame by the stage-coach, and fain was I to be at hame again; and I never sid Dame Crowl o' Applewale, God be thanked, either in appearance or in dream, at-efter.

But when I was grown to be a woman, my aunt spent a day and night wi' me at Littleham, and she telt me there was no doubt it was the poor little boy that was missing sa lang sen, that was shut up to die thar in the dark by that wicked beldame, whar his skirls, or his prayers, or his thumpin' cud na be heard, and his hat was left by the water's edge, whoever did it, to mak' belief he was drowned.

The clothes, at the first touch, a' ran into a snuff o' dust in the cell whar the bayans was found. But there was a handful o' jet buttons, and a knife with a green heft, together wi' a couple o' pennies the poor little fella had in his pocket, I suppose, when he was decoyed in thar, and sid his last o' the light. And there was, amang the squire's papers, a copy o' the notice that was prented after he was lost, when the ald squire thought he might 'a run away, or bin took by gipsies, and it said he had a green-hefted knife wi' him, and that his buttons were o' cut jet. Sa that is a' I hev to say consarnin' ald Dame Crowl, o' Applewale House.

7
The Legend of Dunblane

1.

'IT WAS IN the year 1793,' said my uncle, 'that I made
the acquaintance of William Dunblane, afterwards
Lord Dunblane, at the University of St Andrew's. His
bachelor uncle, the then lord, was not a very rich
man, and he was a stingy one. William's father, too,
was still alive, so that the young man was somewhat
straitened as to money. We were just of an age, and
my father was very liberal to me. Our relative positions, therefore, were more equal at that time than
they afterwards became; and, in spite of the great
difference of rank, Dunblane singled me out to be his
favourite companion. I cannot say why this was,
unless it may have been that I was a more patient
listener than many other young fellows, to his long
stories about his ancestry, and that while I always
endeavoured to tell him the truth, I was more in-
dulgent to this weakness of family pride than the rest
were. They used to laugh at him, at first; but that, he
soon showed them, he would never stand. He was
very strong, and very patriotic; and his face at such
times became as that of one possessed with a devil.'

It was in these words that my uncle, Mr Carthews,
senior partner in the firm of Carthews and Bontor, of
Aberdeen and Calcutta, used generally to begin the
following strange narrative. Like many Scotchmen of
his day, he had a somewhat inordinate reverence for
rank; but it was balanced, in his case, by a
businesslike appreciation of the value of money.
What is of more import, however, to the matter in
hand, was his strict and fearless adherence to the

truth, joined to an extremely kind nature. These characteristics were conspicuous in every transaction of a long life. He was a shrewd, upright man, universally respected in the city where he passed the best part of his life: 'stiff in opinions', occasionally prolix, but of a sound, clear judgment, and unimpeached honesty.

In the narrative, therefore, which I shall try to give, as far as possible in my uncle's own words, there is, I am confident, no wilful misrepresentation, no jot or tittle added to the facts, as he believed them to be. And his opinion of those facts, I take it, was formed very deliberately. I heard him tell the story repeatedly, yet it never varies in the smallest particular; I know it invariably impressed his hearers with a sense of horrible reality. Imagine that the ladies have left the room; three or four men are seated round the polished mahogany; my uncle, a white-haired, keen-eyed man of seventy, bids us draw our chairs nearer the fire, and, passing round a magnum of his fine port, he thus continues the story, of which I have given the opening words, with that incisive Scotch accent, and in that measured phrase, which seems to weigh each word in the balance, and reject it if found wanting.

Dunblane was an unpopular man. Men could not make him out. His manner was often disagreeable, and he was subject to moody fits, when he would speak to no one. He was capable of kind and generous acts, but implacable in his dislikes; and he never forgot an injury. I could manage him better than any one, and he would generally stand the truth from me; but his rage was a terrible thing to witness. I have never seen anything like it. Men used to say, 'Keep clear of Dunblane when the fit is on him; he will stick at nothing.'

The French Revolution was then at its height. Dunblane was a hot royalist, and used to be thrown into fresh transports of fury with the news of every act subversive of the king's authority. One night a man, in my room, who professed Republican sentiments, defended the conduct of the Assembly in imprisoning the royal family. Dunblane got up and flung a bottle at his head. There was a fine row and it was arranged that the two men must fight the next morning. I secretly gave notice to the authorities, however, who interfered, and some sort of peace was patched up; but Dunblane never spoke to his antagonist again as long as he was in the university. I mention this, as I happen to recall the circumstances, just to give you an idea of the man's violence, and of the depth of his resentment.

I can remember, too, a conversation we had one day about marriage. He had been complaining of his poverty, but said that, nevertheless, he meant to marry early.

'You see, it is necessary that I should have an heir, lest the direct line become extinct. There is no one, after me.'

'Do nothing in a hurry,' I replied. 'It would be a great misfortune, no doubt, that the title and estate should pass away to another branch of the family, but it would be a still greater one to have your whole life embittered by an unhappy marriage. You are young; you have life before you. Be quite sure it is for your happiness, ere you take such a step as this.'

His reply was very characteristic.

'Oh,' he said, 'it is all very well for you to talk, who have plenty of money and have no great name as an inheritance. We trace back our descent for six hundred years; it is a duty we owe to the country to keep up the family. If I was fortunate enough to be in your position I should please myself. But, as it is, everything else is of secondary importance. My lord is always telling me so, and I suppose he is right. I must marry a woman with money, and I must have an heir. You don't know,' he added with the black look gathering in his brow, '*how* essential this is.'

I assured him that I fully recognised the obligations which a great name and title entail, but that I could not think that to contract a hasty, ill-considered marriage could ever answer in the long run.

'Ah!' he said. 'Then you have never heard the old prophecy in the family:

When five Dunblanes have had no son,

Then shall the line direct be run.

My uncle is the fourth lord who has had no son. If he should survive my father, and that I should succeed him, I shall be the fifth. You see now how necessary it is I should marry early.'

'On account of a foolish distich!' I replied. His superstition amounted almost to an insanity, and I never would give in to it, though I confess I have known more curious cases of such prophecies being fulfilled than any sceptical Englishman would believe. However, that has nothing to say to the matter in hand. Dunblane repeatedly referred to this prediction, which had evidently taken a hold upon his mind, not to be shaken by any words of mine. He would brood for hours over this and similar subjects. And among them, I have little doubt, was one to which he never referred at that time, seeing that I treated his superstitions with unbecoming levity – a subject of which I had no knowledge for many years afterwards, but which was destined to have a fatal influence on his life.

In '96 I left college and was sent out to our branch house in Calcutta. I heard the following year of Dunblane's marriage to a Miss Cameron, an orphan of good family, though not noble, said to possess both wealth and beauty; and I heard no more. He never wrote to me, nor did I expect it. Our lines of life were now quite different, and though I knew that he would always retain a friendly recollection of me, correspondence was another matter. I was a man of business, and engrossed in affairs of which he could take no interest; while I, on the other hand, knew nothing of the persons and the circumstances by which he was surrounded.

I shall always regret that he did *not* write to me during those years; though probably no written words of mine could have been of any avail in arresting him; but I have occasionally found, in life, that the truth, though discarded at the time, will come back at some unexpected moment and give the devil the lie. Now the devil had it all his own way with Dunblane for years. His father, to whom I think he was really attached, was dead; his uncle, whom he disliked and feared, would not die. The uncle, I am told, proposed this marriage to him, and though Dunblane was indifferent – or more than indifferent – to the lady, he consented to marry her. This was the fatal error which nothing could retrieve. It was the first step down-hill, after which the descent became more and more rapid every year.

In 1803 Lord Dunblane did, at last, die, and a few months later, my own father's death recalled me to Aberdeen where I took his place as head of the house. One day, about a year after my return, George Pilson (you remember Pilson and Pilson, the attorneys? – very respectable firm) was in my office, and chanced to speak of Dunblane Castle, where he had lately been. His father, I found out, was Lord Dunblane's man of business; and I questioned George as to his lordship's present condition and mode of life. His answer was far from satisfactory.

'His Lordship's strangeness and his violent ebullitions of temper have increased very much upon him of late,' he said. 'It is supposed that this is greatly owing to the fact that after nearly eight years of marriage there is no heir to the title. Then his wife is a person singularly unsuited to him in all ways. Her ladyship is handsome, but wanting in common-sense, garrulous in the extreme, laughing immoderately in and out of season, and, if I may be allowed to express an opinion on such a point, deficient in the dignity befitting her station. These things are perpetual blisters, I fancy, to his lordship. Her ladyship, in a word, is what may be called a "provoking woman", and as his lordship is not the most patient of men you may guess the consequences.'

I replied that I was more sorry than surprised: from what I knew of Lord Dunblane I never expected that such a marriage – one purely of interest – could turn out well. 'And yet,' I added, 'if he had fallen into other hands, I think he might have become a very different man. There were germs of good in him.'

At this George Pilson remained silent for few moments, a silence which I thought most eloquent. He then proceeded to speak of the castle, which he described as one of the finest monuments of the fifteenth century remaining in the country.

'His lordship is justly proud of it,' he said, 'though with his pride is mingled a certain superstitious awe, as, no doubt, you know? I dare say he has often spoken to you of the secret room in the castle?'

'No,' I replied, 'I do not remember that he ever did. What is there special about this room?'

He replied, 'No one knows exactly where it is except the owner, the heir, and one other person, who happens, at present, to be my father. The family superstition concerning this room is very strong, and I believe they shrink from speaking of it.'

'But what does it arise from?' I inquired.

He said, 'The legend runs that some former lord of Dunblane sold himself to the devil in this room; the plain English of which is, I imagine, that he committed some foul crime there. At all events, this room has remained shut up for centuries; and it was predicted by one of those sibyls, who were given to such utterances, that, if ever the secret were made known, the ruin of the house would follow.'

'Why,' I exclaimed, 'this is the second prophecy

160

that has been made about the Dunblanes! One pays dearly for belonging to these great families if one is to be subject to all these superstitions. Do you know if the room is ever opened?'

'Yes, I believe so, once a year; when, if possible, the three who are in possession of the secret meet there. My father never speaks on the subject, of course, nor does Lord Dunblane.'

I asked who the heir-in-law was. He told me they had difficulty in finding him out. He was in very poor circumstances, being descended from a younger branch of the Dunblanes, who had gone to settle in England in the beginning of the last century.

After some further conversation, Pilson took his leave, and I thought very little more about Lord Dunblane and his affairs, having concerns of my own which fully occupied my thoughts at that time.

Some weeks later I received, to my surprise, a letter from Lord Dunblane, saying that he had just heard from his man of business, Mr Pilson, that I was returned from India, and living in Aberdeen; and that it would give him great pleasure to see me again, if I would pay him a visit at Dunblane Castle. He named a day when he was expecting a party; but added that if the time was not convenient to me, I could write myself and propose some later date. It would have been ungracious to have refused such an invitation. Indeed, I was fully sensible of the honour, though I anticipated but little pleasure from this visit, under present circumstances. A press of business retained me in Aberdeen just then, but I promised to write, and I did write some weeks later, to his lordship, proposing to accompany Mr Pilson, who informed me he was going to Dunblane Castle: for I reflected that as the stage would take me no further than Nairn, we could share a post-chaise together, which would lighten the cost of the journey, in which business had no part. His lordship replied, in a few lines, to say I should be welcome, and accordingly, on the tenth of April, 1804, Pilson and I left Aberdeen by the stage, which started at six am, and reached Dunblane Castle late that afternoon.

It was getting dusk as we drove up to this magnified remnant of the feudal age – a pile which impressed me with a sense of the power which must have belonged to the Dunblanes in past ages, and heightened their claim to consideration, in my eyes at least, more than the finest modern palace could have done. It was the grandest specimen of this style of architecture I ever saw, of vast extent, its skyline bristling with pointed turrets, its grey walls crowning a steep height covered with venerable Scotch firs, a dry moat surrounding it, and a gateway leading into a courtyard, which occupied nearly an acre, and round which the castle was built.

Lord Dunblane met us in the hall. The nine years which had elapsed since we had parted had wrought changes in us both, no doubt; but in the man I saw before me I should scarcely have recognised my fellow-student had I met him in the streets of Aberdeen. He was grown very large, and on his face, which was lined far beyond his years, the hard, wild look which had been transient formerly, had settled down, apparently into its habitual expression.

He received me kindly, but there was no smile as he shook my hand. The light had died out of the face, never to be rekindled. He told me I should have but a dull visit, he feared. 'Had you come six weeks ago when I wanted you, you would have met a country gathering: not that I like that sort of thing: I hate it; but you and I were always different, Carthews. Now you will find no one; and I have a good deal of business with Mr Pilson, so that I must leave Lady Dunblane to entertain you.' I assured him that I could be perfectly happy, exploring the beauties of the park and adjoining forest, and begged him not to consider me for a moment. After that he led me upstairs to the drawing-room, where Lady Dunblane was seated alone.

The first impression produced in everyone by her ladyship's beauty could not but be favourable. She was a brunette; tall, with lively eyes and brilliant teeth, which she showed a great deal when she laughed, and dark brown hair cut short and dishevelled in loose waves over her head. Upon this occasion, however, I saw nothing but a curl or two; for she wore a species of helmet, much affected, as I afterwards learnt, by women of condition, in that day, whose husbands commanded regiments of yeomanry, as did Lord Dunblane. Being the first head-gear of the kind which I had seen, its singularity struck me, but her ladyship carried this curious erection of buckram, fur and tinsel, with a grace which forbade a thought of ridicule. Her beautiful figure was set off by a spenser of scarlet cloth, and a tight-fitting skirt of some white material which appeared to have been damped, it clung so closely to her person. It was evident her ladyship was not neglectful of her appearance, nor unmindful of the impression she made upon even a humble individual like myself. She came forward and greeted me with infinite suavity, saying:

'It is amiable of you, Mr Carthews, to come and take pity on our solitude. We see no one from one week's end to another in this castle of Otranto (you have read Mr Walpole's romance?) where all is so gloomy and mysterious that, as I tell my lord, I am really alarmed some times at the sound of my own voice!'

'I wish that occurred oftener,' muttered his lordship. She continued, laughing, 'Our only society are the ghosts. You don't mind them, I hope? They are all of the oldest families, for we are mighty select here, you must know. If they visit you, you must esteem it a great honour, Mr Carthews.'

I replied in the same strain, that I felt myself to be wholly unworthy of that honour; but that, if they came, I would try and receive them with becoming courtesy.

'Like my parrot,' cried her ladyship, laughing. 'He and my spaniel sleep in my room; and sometimes, in the dead of night, he calls out, "Pray, come in, and take a chair!" which startles me from my sleep, and frightens me out of my senses!'

His lordship said something about her having no senses to be frightened out of, I believe, and something about 'brutes'. She caught up the word with a laugh.

'Brutes? Oh, yes; one gets accustomed to the society

of brutes of any sort, when one has nothing else all
day.'

Such enmities passed between the two were of
constant occurrence, I suppose, for they produced
little effect beyond deepening the scowl on his
lordship's face. As to me, I felt very uncomfortable,
and the charm of Lady Dunblane's beauty had already
melted away. Though not a stupid woman, I saw she
was a very foolish one. How she dared to aggravate
a man of such a temperament as her husband's amazed
me. It was just like a child handling fire. She rattled
away and laughed that evening with little intermis-
sion. Lord Dunblane scarcely opened his lips. Over
the wine Pilson and I talked; but his lordship stared
moodily into the fire, and said nothing. I began to
think I had made a mistake in coming all the way
from Aberdeen for this. To play the part of chorus to
a matrimonial duet of the most discordant character
was not pleasant; and if my former friend was so
self-absorbed as to be unable to speak to me, the
sooner I left him the better. I suppose something of
this sort struck him, for he said, as he wished me
good night, 'You must not mind my silence and
absence of mind, Carthews. I am very glad to see you
here; but my present position gives me many anxie-
ties. I am irritated and worried until, by Heaven! I
feel at times as if I should go mad.'

Well, I went to bed, and slept soundly. I never was
an imaginative man, you see, or the room I was in
might have conjured up some of those spiritual visi-
tants her ladyship had joked about, evidently to her
lord's annoyance. Not that it was any worse than

165

the other rooms in the castle. I take it they were all oak-panelled, with hideous family portraits grinning from the wall upon vast draperied beds, in one of which I slept without waking, until the servant brought in my hot water for shaving. It was a bright morning, and at breakfast I found my host in better spirits than he seemed the previous evening. I could not help speculating whether this could be in consequence of Lady Dunblane's absence. She never came down to breakfast, I found. Her maid, a most formidable-looking female, with red hair and the muscles of a gillie, came in, I remember, with a tray, and took her ladyship's chocolate up to her. This person, I was afterwards told, had been born on the estate, and was devoted to Dunblane. She had been ill spoken of as a girl; but Dunblane's mother had befriended her and made this Elspie her body servant, and Dunblane had insisted, when he married, on her filling the same office to his wife, much to that lady's annoyance, who wished for a modish waiting-woman from Edinburgh or London. So much for this ill-favoured specimen of her sex to whom I never spoke in my life, but who impressed me very unfavourably whenever I saw her.

After breakfast his lordship took me over the castle, and gave me all the historical associations connected with it, showing me, with great pride, the bed in which Queen Mary had slept, a yew tree said to have been planted by Robert Bruce, and the suit of armour borne by Dunblane of Dunblane at the battle of Bannockburn. He dilated on the glories of his house with more animation that I had yet observed: then suddenly the cloud came over him. 'And to think,' he said, 'that all this must pass into another line – into hands which have been debased by trade (which was not polite to me; but he entirely forgot my presence for the moment, I am sure); 'to think that people who have hardly a drop of old blood in the veins, who have intermarried for generations with Smiths and Browns, and plebeian names of that kind, should come to inherit *this,* which they have no feeling for, no pride in – by God, it is enough to wring one's heart!'

And this was the way he went on, from time to time, bursting out in imprecations on his fate in having no heir, and upon the evil star which had risen over his house. It was in vain that I pointed out that he was young still, and in good health, and must not abandon hope. He shook his head gloomily. 'The prophecy is against me: it is no use.

When five Dunblanes have had no son,
Then shall the line direct be run.

It is clear enough, is it not? I am doomed. I should have known it. When did such a prophecy ever come wrong? What a cursed fool I was to marry!'

So I thought; to marry, that is to say, as he had done; but I abstained from saying so. By-and-by his lordship took Mr Pilson to his study, where they were engaged for some time over business; and I was left alone to ramble about the castle, inside and out, as I would.

Remembering the story I had heard of a secret room, I counted all the windows outside, and then, returning to the castle, traversed every passage, mounted every turret, and opened every door I could, to see if the number of windows corresponded. With the help of the serving man whom I met on the stairs, and who knew all the rooms in the castle, he said, I accounted for each window satisfactorily. And after two hours' diligent endeavour to solve this mystery, I arrived at the conclusion that there was no room – it was all humbug. I was at a time of life, you see, when over-confidence in one's own powers is apt to lead one to very false conclusions.

At luncheon Lady Dunblane appeared, and an incident, which left a painful impression on my mind, took place on that occasion. Dunblane had a peculiar aversion to her ladyship's spaniel. Strict orders were given that he was to be confined to her ladyship's own suite of rooms, and on no account to be allowed beyond them. But some door had inadvertently been left open, and, while we were at luncheon, the spaniel ran barking into the room, round and round the table, and finally straight between his lordship's legs, who was at that moment smarting under one of his wife's sallies. He roared out in a voice of thunder:

'How often have I told you, ma'am, to keep that infernal little beast in your own room?' and he kicked out so viciously, that he sent the poor animal spinning along the oak floor to the further end of the room where he lay howling. His mistress ran up, and seized him in her arms; the creature's leg was broken. Her ladyship shrieked and stamped, and my lord swore; and, thoroughly sickened with the whole scene, I rose and left the room. Pilson joined me in the hall.

'What is to be the end of all this?' I said to him.

His answer was, 'I am afraid to think.'

'Lord Dunblane,' I said, 'seems to me to be losing all self-restraint. If he goes on thus, what will become of him?'

Pilson looked round him, then leaned forward and whispered, 'He will end his days in a madhouse.'

Dunblane shut himself into his room for the rest of the afternoon. By-and-by her ladyship drove out in her coach and four, and carried her dog in her arms to a veterinary surgeon some miles off. At dinner she appeared in as brilliant spirits as ever. How much of this was real I cannot say; nor, supposing her hilarity to be assumed, whether it was done for the purpose of aggravating her lord. It certainly succeeded, if so. His moroseness was enlivened by several ferocious sallies. The conversation turned upon France, I remember, and on the probabilities of the First Consul being made emperor, a subject that engrossed all minds just then.

'How I admire this little man!' exclaimed her ladyship. 'How much greater to found a dynasty, as he is doing, than to inherit all the crowns in Europe! I begin to wish I was a Frenchwoman!'

'I begin to wish you were!' cried my lord. 'There is not another British peeress who would disgrace herself by uttering such a sentiment.'

She laughed aloud, and replied, 'Oh! because they are less frank than I am. All women admire Le Petit Caporal in their hearts. What fun it will be if he comes over here and conquers us! It will be much nicer being the subjects of a great hero instead of the subjects of a mad old king who – '

'Hold your tongue, ma'am!' shouted Dunblane, bringing his fist down upon the table with a force which made the glasses clatter: 'or, if you will talk your low treasonous rubbish, go and talk it in the kitchen. You shall *not* talk it here!'

She only laughed in reply. She certainly seemed to take a delight in provoking him; and, as she knew his sensitive points, this was not difficult. I found an opportunity over a game of cribbage, later in the evening, of asking her why she acted thus. No doubt this was somewhat of a liberty, considering our short acquaintance; but I felt I could not remain longer in the house without trying to amend matters.

'Oh,' she said, 'anything for a little excitement in this horridly monstrous life. I should die of ennui if it wasn't for the tiffs with my lord.'

I told her she did not know what harm she was doing, and I asked if she never felt afraid of irritating a man so passionate as his lordship.

'Bless you, no,' was her reply. 'It is he who is afraid, *really,* of me – of my tongue, you see. Ha, ha! no one ever answered him before, his mother, his servants, his friends, why – you yourself, I dare say, you never contradicted him? Now, I *always* do, and I always say just what I like. He hates me, of course, but he is afraid of me, Mr Carthews. Ha, ha, ha!'

Good heavens! I thought to myself, and these two people are tied to each other for life. Both have a fair chance of living for the next forty years. What a prospect! Even before we separated for the night she had stung him with another of her irritating speeches. There had been some talk of the steward's boy, who

'... A figure glided forth and ran swiftly towards the well ...'

(see p. 177)

had tumbled from a tree, and had broken his leg. . . . 'Children are a horrid bore,' said Lady Dunblane. 'Thank Heaven, I have no brat to be tumbling from trees, and worrying one's life out.'

I dare say she did not mean it. It is hardly possible that, under the circumstances, she should not have wished for a child. The devil was in the woman, constantly prompting something to aggravate her husband. His back was towards me, on this occasion, and, he said nothing, so I could only judge of the effect produced upon him by his instantly lighting a chamber candlestick and leaving the room. We saw no more of him that night.

The next day and the day following only further developed the hopeless condition of affairs between Lord and Lady Dunblane. I tried once to speak to him on the subject, but I found it was in vain. An ineradicable hatred of his wife had grown up in him, which he did not attempt to conceal. When alone with him, he would occasionally converse; in her presence he seemed to be perpetually on the look-out for what might drop from her irrepressible tongue. The fourth day of my stay at the castle – the day before I was obliged to return to Aberdeen – arrived, and with it a guest, who, although expected, was evidently anything but welcome. This was Mr James Dunblane, the heir-in-law, who had only lately been traced, and between whom and Lord Dunblane certain communications had passed by letter. This was his first visit to the castle – a visit which, as I afterwards learnt, was a matter almost of necessity. He seemed to feel the awkwardness of his position. I do not remember much about the young man, except that he was plain in person and very quiet. Lord Dunblane received him coldly, but politely. Lady Dunblane, after the usual fashion, plunged at once into the subject of all others his lordship shrank from any notice of.

'So you are come, as heir-in-law, to be let into the secret of this famous room, are you? Why, it is as bad as being made a freemason!. ... Can you keep a secret, Mr Dunblane? because, if not, untold misfortunes are to befall us.' And the laugh with which she concluded sounded to me like the screech of an owl forboding evil. Lord Dunblane looked as if he could have stabbed her, but he only muttered an oath under his breath, and clenched his fist – a movement which no one saw but myself. Every incident of that evening is fresh in my recollection. I remember how she returned again and again to that subject, as though it had a fatal fascination for her, but more likely, I fear, because she saw that her husband writhed under it. She ridiculed the prophecy, and laughed at all those superstitions, which his lordship cherished as his religion. It was distressing to watch him the while. He was far quieter than usual, scarcely spoke, but sat, his arms crossed, staring at the fire, with eyes which burnt, themselves, like coals, and when he swore, which he did once or twice, it was in a suppressed voice, contrasting strangely with his usual violence. But there was a vibration in the tone which showed how strongly he was stirred. At last, it was late in the evening, and we were sitting round her ladyship's tea-table, when she committed her crowning act of folly by offering to lay a wager with any one that she would find out the secret room herself. I need hardly say no one accepted the challenge. But she was not to be discouraged. She had seen her husband's face go white, and the look which he shot at her gave a zest to her audacious schemes. She repeated her declaration that she would penetrate this wonderful mystery. Such things were well enough to frighten old women with in the middle ages, but how any one could believe in predictions and other rubbish of this kind in the present day passed her comprehension. For her part she had no faith in anything of the kind, and to prove what folly it was, she should leave no stone unturned to discover this room about which such a fuss was made: after which the secret, she declared, should remain one no longer.

I tried to stop her: it was all no use. She had got the bit between her teeth, so to speak, and away she went, partly to show off, and partly out of spite, regardless what she said, provided it produced an effect and inflamed my lord yet more. She pictured, laughingly, the cobwebbed condition of the room, and how she would turn in the housemaid with broom and duster: after which she would give an evening party there, and invite all the ghosts to come, if they chose – 'indeed the black gentleman himself!'. . . . Poor man, she little knew what she was invoking. No one laughed. Even the heir who, being shy, always smiled when required, looked too stupefied to comply with the demand on this occasion. To glance at Lord Dunblane's face was enough to check any inclination to hilarity. I have never forgotten its expression. I had witnessed his ungovernable passion scores of times, prompting him to sudden acts of violence. But now, there was a certain admixture of *fear* (she had divined rightly, I saw, when she said he was afraid of her) with the rage which trembled through his whole frame, the like of which I have never beheld but once since in my life. I saw a beast-tamer enter the hyenas' den at the show last year. The aspect of their malignant fury cowed by terror, but watching for its opportunity to burst forth, the savage hissing wherewith they received the lash and showed their fangs, recalled to me Dunblane's demeanour as he listened to his wife. . . . At last, I could stand it no longer, and made up my mind to tell a lie.

'Lady Dunblane,' I said, 'like most Scotchmen, I am a trifle superstitious. This is my last night under your hospitable roof, and I am sure you would not willingly disturb its rest. You are so happily constituted as to be above fear of any kind. Others are weaker. Let me earnestly advise you to leave all superstitions connected with Dunblane Castle alone. Believe me, "there are more things in heaven and earth than are dreamt of in your ladyship's philosophy".'

She burst out a-laughing, as usual. 'Oh, Mr Carthews, I'm ashamed of you. But I see what it is. You are afraid, not of the ghosts and the predictions, but of my lord. Well, I shall see you in May, when I pass through Aberdeen on my way south, and I shall tell you all about it then; for depend upon it, I shall have found out the secret by that time.'

175

And so, in the insolence of youth and high spirits and an indomitable will, she bade me good-night, poor woman, and I never saw her again.

Dunblane had left the room. Whether it was pre-arranged that Pilson and the young heir were to join him in his study, and that later in the night the door of the secret room should be unlocked, I know not. I am inclined, from one or two circumstances, to think that it was so; but, again, there were other things which have made me doubt it. At all events, when we three had bid each other good-night, neither Pilson nor young Dunblane dropped anything which should lead me to suppose they were not going straight to their own rooms. They were not to leave the castle till the day after me. It was quite possible, therefore, that the chamber was to be unlocked after my departure.

2.

I slept soundly the first part of the night. But about three o'clock I woke suddenly – I might almost say, I started from my sleep. I had not been dreaming; I was not conscious of having heard any noise; but my sleep, somehow or other, was broken suddenly and I sat up in bed with a sense of undefined alarm. I listened: all was still – the soughing of the wind among the Scotch firs below the rampart-wall was the only thing I heard. But, feeling restless, I jumped out of bed, went to the window and opened it. There was no moon, but it was a light night. I could distinguish the ivy on the wall beneath, the little door in the angle of the turret opposite, and the dusky forms of the owls that flew past the window. Almost immediately beneath was a curious old well said to be of wonderful depth, but long since unused. If one dropped a stone in there an interval which seemed like half a minute elapsed before a faint splash told that it had reached the bottom.

I had been at the window a few minutes when the door in the turret opposite opened, with a slight grating sound which attracted my attention. A figure glided forth, and then ran swiftly towards the well. I distinguished that it was a woman by the long drapery, and as she came under the window I could just make out that she carried some sort of vessel in her hand. Whatever it was she threw it in, and waited, leaning over the side, until she caught the distant thud of the object as it met the water. Then she returned rather more leisurely than she had come, the door was shut, and, though I waited at the window a full hour, I saw and heard no more.

I do not know that at any other place, at any other time, this circumstance would have aroused my curiosity. As it was, I could not get to sleep again for thinking of it, and speculating what could have been the motive that induced any female of the establishment to rise in the dead of night in order to cast something into the well.

I had to be stirring very early, and I was at my solitary breakfast when Lord Dunblane entered. He looked ghastly, so much so that I could not help asking if he was. He turned fiercely round upon me, demanding why I asked.

'Because you look as if you had not slept,' I said.

'And you? Pray how did you sleep?' he inquired, knitting his brows. 'You were not disturbed? You had no nightmare after Lady Dunblane's conversation last night?'

I had resolved to say nothing of what I had seen, and replied that I had rested pretty well. I was then proceeding to express my thanks to him for his hospitality when he interrupted me. 'If you wish to show yourself a friend, say as little as possible about your visit here to anyone. I am going abroad at once. I have made up my mind that Lady Dunblane can live here no longer. You have heard enough to know that she hates the place – and it disagrees with her, moreover. She has had several epileptic attacks – a severe one this very night; it is evident that the climate does not suit her, and I am recommended to take her to Italy. My lady and I can never agree here. She does all she can to goad me to madness – and perhaps she has succeeded: who can say? People will gossip, Carthews, when we are gone. Prove yourself a friend, and say nothing about our quarrels while you have been here.'

I was a good deal surprised at the tenor of his speech, but thought it reasonable upon the whole. There was something in his eye, nevertheless, which disquieted me. Coupling it with Pilson's words, two days previously, and with my own observations, I could not avoid the conviction that the fate to which he himself had just now alluded was imminent. It might be warded off, perhaps, by change of scene, and the removal of the causes of irritation, but it was impossible to look at him steadily, and to doubt that

178

incipient insanity was there. I begged him to act upon his determination of going abroad without loss of time; and then, shaking his hand, I stepped into the chaise, and drove off.

Well, I returned to Aberdeen; and some days after this Pilson called on me. I asked what news he brought of Lord and Lady Dunblane.

'They are gone abroad. I suppose it is the best thing he could do. Her ladyship had a succession of such severe fits that she was unable to leave her room, or to see anyone but her maid after you left. I did see her once at the window, and her look quite alarmed me. His lordship was much calmer, but he scarcely spoke. His wife's sudden prostration, after all their violent bickerings, affected him a good deal. He is in a bad way, I think, Carthews. I mean that I am very much afraid –' and he pointed significantly to his head.

I told him I fully shared his apprehensions, and then asked him more particularly to describe the change in Lady Dunblane's appearance.

'The morning I left I was walking round the rampart when I heard one of the windows rattle. I looked up, and there was Lady Dunblane, her head pressed against the panes, and with such a terrible expression of agony in her face as I shall never forget. She kept opening her mouth, and making the most hideous grimaces at me, so that it was clear she was not quite in her right senses at the moment. She disappeared suddenly.'

'Did you ever see any indication of a tendency to such a malady in her ladyship?' I asked.

'No. I cannot say I ever did,' he replied.

'Was the doctor sent for?'

'Yes, the country apothecary came once.'

'And what did he say? Did you speak to him?'

'Yes. I saw him in the hall as he was stepping into his buggy. I asked him how he found her ladyship. He said she was much prostrated by the violence of the attack, but he seemed a puzzle-headed fellow. No doubt he was awed by the honour of being sent for to the castle; for I could not get much out of him. He seemed dazed; but muttered something about change being good for her ladyship.'

'And who attended her during these attacks?' I inquired.

'No one but his lordship and the maid Elspie. My lord told me that his wife was very violent; but he would not suffer any of the men to be sent for, to hold her. He and Elspie, who is a very powerful woman, managed her between themselves. He said that he had found it necessary to tie her hands. I do not envy him his journey. They left in the family coach an hour after our departure, and were to travel night and day to Leith, where they took ship for Holland.'

He then went on to say that the young heir-in-law had returned to London much depressed with his visit, and that the necessary formalities having now been gone through (which I understood to mean that the secret of the haunted room had been duly communicated to him) Mr Dunblane would in all probability never see the castle again during my lord's lifetime.

I seldom saw Pilson for some time after this conversation; when I did, he told me what little he knew
of the Dunblanes; but months often elapsed without
his having any direct communication with my lord,
and even then the letters received were mere bald
statements and inquiries, exclusively upon matters of
business. These, however, were sufficient to show that
his mind had not given way; they were lucid and
perspicacious in every detail. There was never any
mention of her ladyship; for the obvious reason, as it
transpired after a while, that she and my lord were
separated. He was travelling now in Italy, now in
Hungary, now in the East, while she remained – no
one knew exactly where – in Switzerland. At the end
of the third year he returned to Dunblane, and shut
himself up there, refusing to see any of the neighbours who called. In reply to every inquiry for her
ladyship (more especially those which a distant
cousin, her only relation, made about this time), he
stated that her ladyship's health obliged her to remain
on the Continent; her mind had been much weakened
by continued epileptic attacks, and she was unequal to
correspondence. He stated, further, that she was
under excellent medical care and that, though, by
reason of the excitement under which she sometimes
laboured, it was not deemed advisable that he should
visit her often, he made a point of doing so once a
year. This statement seems to have been considered
satisfactory. Lady Dunblane's friends – and she had
very few – were not suspicious, and the world at
large troubled itself but little with the domestic
concerns of a couple who had lived in isolated gran-

deur, with rare exceptions, since his lordship's accession to the title. Pilson went twice to the castle, during that year, and, as far as I know, he was the only guest. He gave a gloomy picture of the solitary man shut up in that big place. We both avoided all mention of her ladyship's name; but I now know that he was no easier than I was on that head.

It was towards the close of 1808 that he called on me one morning, at an unusually early hour. His face, his whole manner, betokened that my grave, quiet friend was unusually perturbed. He looked round the room – this very room where we are sitting – drew his chair close to mine, and said in a whisper:

'Carthews, I have come to you in a very distressing emergency. I hardly know whether I am justified in taking this step, but I do know that I can depend on you, and you may materially help me in a most painful and difficult situation.'

Without more ado, he then proceeded to say that a young Frenchman, who gave his name as Jean Marcel, had called upon him the previous night, stating that he had lately come from Geneva, where he was in a wine merchant's office, and had been sent on business to Aberdeen. He was the bearer of a small crumpled note, addressed in nearly illegible characters, to M Pilson, Attorney, Aberdeen. He stated that he had come by it thus. Shortly before leaving Geneva, it had been his duty to inspect the 'recolte' of various vineyards: among them one belonging to the Chateau d'Osman some miles distant. The house itself was tenanted by an English lady, who was said to be mad or imbecile. At all

182

events she was never heard to speak, and was closely watched by her attendants night and day. She walked on a terrace overlooking the vineyard, but it was never out of sight of a gaunt woman, who was, no doubt, her keeper. The intendant of the estate, who told Jean Marcel these particulars, walked through the vineyard with him, when they saw the unhappy lady on the terrace above. Her appearance had much interested Marcel. He described her as a handsome woman, but with a fixed, woe-begone expression of face, and wearing a black cloak, which entirely concealed her person. In the course of Marcel's inspection, they stood for some time just under the terrace wall, and he spoke to the intendant of his approaching visit to Aberdeen. There was no doubt but that he was overheard by the lady on the terrace. She disappeared, but a quarter of an hour later, while they were still near the wall, the two men heard the sound of a running footstep upon the terrace, followed by a plaintive moaning, like that of a wounded bird. They looked up, and there she stood, glancing round with an expression of terror to see if she was followed, and of earnest supplication towards the two men beneath. She opened her mouth wide – a clear proof, the intendant seemed to think, of the poor creature's imbecility – then raised both arms up high, when, to his horror, he perceived that she had lost her right hand. With her left she then suddenly dropped over the wall a paper with a stone inside, and had scarcely done this when her gaunt attendant appeared on the terrace. The poor lady's whole demeanour changed; the old fixed look returned, and she began once more, with slow uncertain steps, to pace the terrace. To satisfy her, Marcel picked up the paper, and pocketed it, as he walked away. As soon as he was out of sight he examined it.

Outside was scrawled, 'Pour l'amour de Dieu remettez cette lettre à son adresse.' Within was the note addressed to Pilson. The intendant laughed at this, and tried to persuade Marcel to tear up the note. 'All mad people imagine themselves to be sane, and this one no doubt wants to persuade her friends that she is unjustly confined; but you need only look at her to see that she is a lunatic.'

Marcel admitted the probability of this, but he could not bring himself to destroy the paper. Whether she was mad or not, the condition of this maimed unhappy creature had aroused his compassion so deeply, that he declared the first thing he would do on arriving at Aberdeen would be to find out the person to whom the note was addressed. And he had done so.

When he had finished this strange narrative, Pilson laid before me a scrap of paper – evidently the blank page torn out of the end of a book – on which was scrawled:

> 'Help! For God's sake, help! before
> they kill me. Oh, save me, Mr Pilson,
> save me, as you hope to be saved hereafter.
> E Dunblane.'

We looked at each other for some minutes without speaking. At last Pilson said:

'If I consulted my own interest, I should remain silent, or simply enclose these lines to his lordship.

Her ladyship's condition, no doubt, justifies any steps that have been taken. I cannot suspect my lord; and if he discovers that I have interfered in his domestic concerns, he will certainly take the management of his affairs out of my hands. But, on the other hand, does not humanity call for some investigation into this? I could not die at peace, remembering that I had turned a deaf ear to such a cry; but I am puzzled what to do, Mr Carthews. It has occurred to me that you may have business connexions with Geneva, and might, perhaps, make inquiries which would not compromise you as they would me.'

In other words, Pilson was anxious to ease his conscience at as little risk to himself as might be. I did not blame him; my interest was too deeply stirred for me not to follow up the inquiry with the keenest avidity. But then, as Pilson had hinted, it is true that I had nothing to lose. I promised him that I would write that very day to a correspondent in Geneva, and desire him to leave no stone unturned towards discovering the truth.

I had to wait some weeks for the answer. The commission was one the execution of which was beset with difficulties. The village pasteur, the doctor, the intendant of the vineyards, and all the neighbours were applied to, but little additional information could be gathered. At last the maire of the district was induced to investigate the case, upon representations being made to him that there existed suspicions as to the treatment which the incarcerated lady – whether insane or only imbecile – met with. After a vigorous resistance they forced an entry into the chateau. The sight that met them was heart-rending. The poor creature lay dying, and but for this intervention would have been denied the last consolations of religion. When the pasteur knelt down, however, and questioned her, she only shook her head and moaned. Then, with an effort, she opened her mouth wide and, to their horror, they perceived that *she had no tongue.*

They implored her to write down the name of the perpetrator of this barbarous crime. But either she had no strength, or else she was praying, poor soul, for grace to forgive her persecutors, rather than retribution. She listened devoutly to the good pasteur's prayers, and with a glorious smile lighted up her tear-worn eyes as the death-film gathered over them. So the unhappy lady passed away. The woman Elspie was, of course, seized, and subjected to a rigorous cross-examination. She declared that the lady who was just dead had been thus mutilated by her husband one night when goaded into a state of insane rage by his wife's discovery of a secret, to which he attached a superstitious importance, and which she threatened to proclaim to all the world. In the struggle to defend herself, her right wrist was also severed. The woman maintained that her mistress had ever since been subject to violent fits of delirium, necessitating restraint. This I do not believe; there is no proof of it whatever. How far the rest of her story was true, it was impossible to say, and will never now be known. There were probabilities in favour of it; but, on the other hand, might not this wretch herself have been the instrument? I did not forget that I had seen her (as I have now no sort of doubt) on that fatal

186

night stealing out to throw *something* into the well. Of her complicity, at all events, there was ample proof, since from the first she was the attendant upon her ill-fated mistress. But the hand of justice, for all that, was stayed.

The very same day that I received the letter containing the foregoing particulars, and while Pilson and I were deliberating what steps must now be taken, the news of an appalling catastrophe, which had happened thirty-six hours previously, reached us. Lord Dunblane had been burnt in his bed, and the greater part of the castle destroyed. How the fire originated was never known, but it broke out from his lordship's room in the dead of night, and three sides of the quadrangle were burnt to the ground before the flames could be got under. The lovers of coincidences tried afterwards to make out that Lord Dunblane and his wife died the same night; the superstitious even fabricated a theory that, struck with remorse, upon learning, by second sight, of his wife's death, he had himself fired the castle, and resolutely perished in the flames. But all this is purely imaginary. It is sufficiently remarkable that these deaths should have been so near one another; but Lady Dunblane died at least five days before her husband; and as to the supposition of his lordship's self-destruction, the only ground for it was his strange mental condition, which was no worse than it had been for the last five years.

The woman Elspie was set at large by the authorities at Geneva, no one coming forward as her accuser. Mr Pilson thought, and I believe he was right, that now both Lord and Lady Dunblane were dead it was better this terrible story should not be made public. It oozed out, in the course of time, as almost all such scandals do, but not through me. It was only when I found that all sorts of false or garbled versions of the circumstances were current in society that I ever mentioned what I knew, and that was years afterwards, when, in default of heirs, the title of Dunblane had become extinct.

8
Green Tea

PROLOGUE

Martin Hesselius, the German Physician

THOUGH CAREFULLY EDUCATED in medicine and surgery, I have never practised either. The study of each continues, nevertheless, to interest me profoundly. Neither idleness nor caprice caused my seccession from the honourable calling which I had just entered. The cause was a very trifling scratch inflicted by a dissecting knife. This trifle cost me the loss of two fingers, amputated promptly, and the more painful loss of my health, for I have never been quite well since, and have seldom been twelve months together in the same place

In my wanderings I became acquainted with Dr Martin Hesselius, a wanderer like myself, like me a physician, and like me an enthusiast in his profession. Unlike me in this, that his wanderings were voluntary, and he a man, if not of fortune, as we estimate fortune in England, at least in what our forefathers used to term 'easy circumstances.' He was an old man when I first saw him; nearly five-and-thirty years my senior.

In Dr Martin Hesselius, I had found my master. His knowledge was immense, his grasp of a case was an intuition. He was the very man to inspire a young enthusiast, like me, with awe and delight. My admiration has stood the test of time and survived the separation of death. I am sure it was well-founded.

For nearly twenty years I acted as his medical secretary. His immense collection of papers he has left in my care, to be arranged, indexed and bound. His treatment of some of these cases is curious. He writes in two distinct characters. He describes what he saw and heard as an intelligent layman might, and when in his style of narrative he had seen the patient either through his own hall-door, to the light of day, or through the gates of darkness to the caverns of the dead, he returns upon the narrative, and in the terms of his art and with all the force and originality of genius, proceeds to the work of analysis, diagnosis and illustration.

Here and there a case strikes me as of a kind to amuse or horrify a lay reader with an interest quite different from the peculiar one which it may possess for an expert. With slight modifications, chiefly of language, and of course a change of names, I copy the following. The narrator is Dr Martin Hesselius. I find it among the voluminous notes of cases which he made during a tour in England about sixty-four years ago.

It is related in series of letters to his friend Professor Van Loo of Leyden. The professor was not a physician, but a chemist, and a man who read history and metaphysics and medicine, and had, in his day, written a play.

The narrative is therefore, if somewhat less valuable as a medical record, necessarily written in a manner more likely to interest an unlearned reader.

These letters, from a memorandum attached, appear to have been returned on the death of the professor, in 1819, to Dr Hesselius. They are written, some in English, some in French, but the greater part in German. I am a faithful, though I am conscious, by no means a graceful translator, and although here and there I omit some passages, and shorten others, and disguise names, I have interpolated nothing.

I.

Dr Hesselius Relates how He Met the Rev Mr Jennings

The Rev Mr Jennings is tall and thin. He is middle-aged, and dresses with a natty, old-fashioned, high church precision. He is naturally a little stately, but not at all stiff. His features, without being handsome, are well formed, and their expression extremely kind, but also shy.

I met him one evening at Lady Mary Heyduke's. The modesty and benevolence of his countenance are extremely prepossessing.

We are but a small party, and he joined agreeably enough in the conversation, He seems to enjoy listening very much more than contributing to the talk; but what he says is always to the purpose and well said. He is a great favourite of Lady Mary's, who it seems, consults him upon many things, and thinks him the most happy and blessed person on earth. Little knows she about him.

The Rev Mr Jennings is a bachelor, and has, they say sixty thousand pounds in the funds. He is a charitable man. He is most anxious to be actively employed in his sacred profession, and yet though always tolerably well elsewhere, when he goes down to his vicarage in Warwickshire, to engage in the actual duties of his sacred calling, his health soon fails him, and in a very strange way. So says Lady Mary.

There is no doubt that Mr Jennings' health does break down in, generally, a sudden and mysterious way, sometimes in the very act of officiating in his old and pretty church at Kenlis. It may be his heart, it may be his brain. But so it has happened three or four times, or oftener, that after proceeding a certain way in the service, he has on a sudden stopped short, and after a silence, apparently quite unable to resume, he has fallen into solitary, inaudible prayer, his hands and his eyes uplifted, and then pale as death, and in the agitation of a strange shame and horror, descended trembling, and got into the vestry-room, leaving his congregation, without explanation, to themselves. This occurred when his curate was absent. When he goes down to Kenlis now, he always takes care to provide a clergyman to share his duty, and to supply his place on the instant should he become thus suddenly incapacitated.

When Mr Jennings breaks down quite, and beats a retreat from the vicarage, and returns to London, where, in a dark street off Piccadilly, he inhabits a very narrow house, Lady Mary says that he is always perfectly well. I have my own opinion about that. There are degrees of course. We shall see.

Mr Jennings is a perfectly gentlemanlike man. People, however, remark something odd. There is an impression a little ambiguous. One thing which certainly contributes to it, people I think don't remember; or, perhaps, distinctly remark. But I did, almost immediately. Mr Jennings has a way of looking sidelong upon the carpet, as if his eye followed the movements of something there. This, of course, not always. It occurs now and then. But often enough to give a certain oddity, as I have said, to his manner, and in this glance travelling along the floor there is something both shy and anxious.

A medical philosopher, as you are good enough to call me, elaborating theories by the aid of cases sought out by himself, and by him watched and scrutinised with more time at command, and consequently infinitely more minuteness that the ordinary practitioner can afford, falls insensibly into habits of observation, which accompany him everywhere, and are exercised, as some people would say, impertinently, upon every subject that presents itself with the least likelihood of rewarding inquiry.

There was a promise of this kind in the slight, timid, kindly, but reserved gentleman, whom I met for the first time at this agreeable little evening gathering. I observed, of course, more than I here set down; but I reserve all that borders on the technical for a strictly scientific paper.

I may remark, that when I here speak of medical science, I do so, as I hope some day to see it more generally understood, in a much more comprehensive sense than its generally material treatment would warrant. I believe the entire natural world is but the ultimate expression of that spiritual world from which, and in which alone, it has its life. I believe that the essential man is a spirit, that the spirit is an organised substance, but as different in point of material from what we ordinarily understand by matter, as light or electricity is; that the material body is, in the most literal sense, a vesture, and death consequently no interruption of the living man's existence, but simply his extrication from the natural body – a process which commences at the moment of what we term death, and the completion of which, at furthest a few days later, is the resurrection 'in power'.

The person who weighs the consequences of these positions will probably see their practical bearing upon medical science. This is, however, by no means the proper place for displaying the proofs and discussing the consequences of this too generally unrecognized state of facts.

In pursuit of my habit, I was covertly observing Mr Jennings, with all my caution – I think he perceived it – and I saw plainly that he was as cautiously observing me. Lady Mary happening to address me by my name, as Dr Hesselius, I saw that he glanced at me more sharply, and then became thoughtful for a few minutes.

After this, as I conversed with a gentleman at the other end of the room, I saw him look at me more steadily, and with an interest which I thought I understood. I then saw him take an opportunity of chatting with Lady Mary, and was, as one always is, perfectly aware of being the subject of a distant inquiry and answer.

This tall clergyman approached me by-and-by; and in a little time we had got into conversation. When two people, who like reading, and know books and places, having travelled, wish to converse, it is very strange if they can't find topics. It was not accident that brought him near me, and led him into conversation. He knew German and had read my Essays on Metaphysical Medicine which suggest more than they actually say.

This courteous man, gentle, shy, plainly a man of thought and reading, who moving and talking among us, was not altogether of us, and whom I already suspected of leading a life whose transactions and alarms were carefully concealed, with an impenetrable reserve from, not only the world, but his best beloved friends – was cautiously weighing in his own mind the idea of taking a certain step with regard to me.

I penetrated his thoughts without his being aware of it, and was careful to say nothing which could betray to his sensitive vigilance my suspicions respecting his position, or my surmises about his plans respecting myself.

We chatted upon indifferent subjects for a time; but at last he said:

'I was very much interested by some papers of yours, Dr Hesselius, upon what you term Metaphysical Medicine – I read them in German, ten or twelve years ago – have they been translated?'

'No, I'm sure they have not – I should have heard. They would have asked my leave, I think.'

'I asked the publishers here, a few months ago, to get the book for me in the original German; but they tell me it is out of print.'

'So it is, and has been for some years; but it flatters

me as an author to find that you have not forgotten my little book, although,' I added, laughing, 'ten or twelve years is a considerable time to have managed without it; but I suppose you have been turning the subject over again in your mind, or something has happened lately to revive your interest in it.'

At this remark, accompanied by a glance of in-quiry, a sudden embarrassment disturbed Mr Jennings, analogous to that which makes a young lady blush and look foolish. He dropped his eyes, and folded his hands together uneasily, and looked oddly, and you would have said, guiltily, for a moment.

I helped him out of his awkwardness in the best way, by appearing not to observe it, and going straight on, I said: 'Those revivals of interest in a subject happen to me often; one book suggests another, and often sends me back a wild-goose chase over an interval of twenty years. But if you will care to possess a copy, I shall be only to happy to provide you; I have still got two or three by me – and if you allow me to present one I shall be very much honoured.'

'You are very good indeed,' he said, quite at his ease again, in a moment: 'I almost despaired – I don't know how to thank you.'

'Pray don't say a word; the thing is really so little worth that I am only ashamed of having offered it, and if you thank me any more I shall throw it into the fire in a fit of modesty.'

Mr Jennings laughed. He inquired where I was staying in London, and after a little more conversation on a variety of subjects, he took his departure.

2.

The Doctor Questions Lady Mary, and She Answers

'I like your vicar so much, Lady Mary,' said I, as soon as he was gone. 'He has read, travelled, and thought, and having also suffered, he ought to be an accomplished companion.'

'So he is, and, better still, he is a really good man,' said she. 'His advice is invaluable about my schools, and all my little undertakings at Dawlbridge, and he's so painstaking, he takes so much trouble – you have no idea – wherever he thinks he can be of use: he's so good-natured and so sensible.'

'It is pleasant to hear so good an account of his neighbourly virtues. I can only testify to his being an agreeable and gentle companion, and in addition to what you have told me, I think I can tell you two or three things about him,' said I.

'Really!'

'Yes, to begin with, he's unmarried.'

'Yes, that's right – go on.'

'He has been writing, that is he *was,* but two or three years perhaps he has not gone on with his work, and the book was upon some rather abstract subject – perhaps theology.'

'Well, he was writing a book, as you say; I'm not quite sure what it was about, but only that it was nothing that I cared for; very likely you are right, and he certainly did stop – yes.'

'And although he only drank a little coffee here

198

to-night, he likes tea, at least, did like it extra-
vagantly.'

'Yes, that's *quite* true.'

'He drank green tea, a good deal, didn't he?' I
pursued.

'Well, that's very odd! Green tea was a subject on
which we used almost to quarrel.'

'But he has quite given that up,' said I.

'So he has.'

'And, now, one more fact. His mother or his father,
did you know them?'

'Yes, both; his father is only ten years dead, and
their place is near Dawlbridge. We knew them very
well,' she answered.

'Well, either his mother or his father – I should
rather think his father, saw a ghost,' said I.

'Well, you really are a conjurer, Dr Hesselius.'

'Conjurer or no, haven't I said right?' I answered
merrily.

'You certainly have, and it *was* his father; he was
a silent, whimsical man, and he used to bore my
father about his dreams, and at last he told him a
story about a ghost he had seen and talked with, and
a very odd story it was. I remember it particularly,
because I was so afraid of him. This story was long
before he died – when I was quite a child – and his
ways were so silent and moping, and he used to drop
in sometimes, in the dusk, when I was alone in the
drawing-room, and I used to fancy there were ghosts
about him.'

I smiled and nodded.

'And now, having established my character as a

199

conjurer, I think I must say good-night,' said I.

'But how *did* you find it out?'

'By the planets, of course, as the gipsies do,' I answered, and so, gaily, we said goodnight.

Next morning I sent the little book he had been inquiring after, and a note to Mr Jennings, and on returning late that evening, I found that he had called at my lodgings, and left his card. He asked whether I was at home, and asked at what hour he would be most likely to find me.

Does he intend opening his case, and consulting me 'professionally,' as they say? I hope so. I have already conceived a theory about him. It is supported by Lady Mary's answers to my parting questions. I should like much to ascertain from his own lips. But what can I do consistently with good breeding to invite a confession? Nothing. I rather think he meditates one. At all events, my dear Val L, I shan't make myself difficult of access; I mean to return his visit tomorrow. It will be only civil in return for his politeness, to ask to see him. Perhaps something may come of it. Whether much, little, or nothing, my dear Van L, you shall hear.

3.

Dr Hesselius Picks up Something in Latin Books

Well, I have called at Blank Street.

On inquiring at the door, the servant told me that

Mr Jennings was engaged very particularly with a gentleman, a clergyman from Kenlis, his parish in the country. Intending to reserve my privilege, and to call again, I merely intimated that I should try another time, and had turned to go, when the servant begged my pardon, and asked me, looking at me a little more attentively than well-bred persons of his order usually do, whether I was Dr Hesselius; and, on learning that I was, he said, 'Perhaps then, sir, you would allow me to mention it to Mr Jennings, for I am sure he wishes to see you.'

The servant returned in a moment, with a message from Mr Jennings, asking me to go into his study, which was in effect his back drawing-room, promising to be with me in a very few minutes.

This was really a study – almost a library. The room was lofty, with two tall slender windows, and rich dark curtains. It was much larger than I had expected, and stored with books on every side, from the floor to the ceiling. The upper carpet – for to my tread it felt that there were two or three – was a Turkey carpet. My steps fell noiselessly. The bookcases standing out, placed the windows, particularly narrow ones, in deep recesses. The effect of the room was, although extremely comfortable, and even luxurious, decidedly gloomly, and aided by the silence, almost oppressive. Perhaps, however, I ought to have allowed something for association. My mind had connected peculiar ideas with Mr Jennings. I stepped into this perfectly silent room, of a very silent house, with a peculiar foreboding; and its darkness, and solemn clothing of books, for except where two narrow looking-glasses were set in the wall, they were everywhere, helped this sombre feeling.

While awaiting Mr Jennings' arrival, I amused myself by looking into some of the books with which his shelves were laden. Not among these, but immediately under them, with their backs upward, on the floor, I lighted upon a complete set of Swedenborg's *Arcana Cælestia,* in the original Latin, a very fine folio set, bound in the natty livery which theology affects, pure vellum, namely, gold letters, and carmine edges. There were paper markers in several of these volumes. I raised and placed them, one after the other upon the table, and opening where these papers were placed, I read in the solemn Latin phraseology, a series of sentences indicated by a pencilled line at the margin. Of these I copy here a few, translating them into English.

'When man's interior sight is opened, which is that of his spirit, then there appear the things of another life, which cannot possibly be made visible to the bodily sight. . . .'

'By the internal sight it has been granted me to see the things that are in the other life, more clearly than I see those that are in the world. From these considerations, it is evident that external vision exists from interior vision, and this from a vision still more interior, and so on. . . .'

'There are with every man at least two evil spirits. . . .'

'With wicked genii there is also a fluent speech, but harsh and grating. There is also among them a speech which is not fluent, wherein the dissent of the thoughts is perceived as something secretly creeping along within it. . . .'

'The evil spirits associated with man are indeed from the hells, but when with man they are not then in hell, but are taken out thence. The place where they then are, is in the midst between heaven and hell, and is called the world of spirits – when the evil spirits who are with man, are in that world, they are not in any infernal torment, but in every thought and affection of man, and so, in all that the man himself enjoys. But when they are remitted into their hell, they return to their former state. . . .'

'If evil spirits could perceive that they were associated with man, and yet that they were spirits separate from him, and if they could flow in into the things of his body, they would attempt by a thousand means to destroy him; for they hate man with a deadly hatred. . . .'

'Knowing, therefore, that I was a man in the body, they were continually striving to destroy me, not as to the body only, but especially as to the soul; for to destroy any man or spirit is the very delight of the life of all who are in hell; but I have been continually protected by the Lord. Hence it appears how dangerous it is for man to be in a living consort with spirits unless he be in the good of faith. . . .'

Nothing is more carefully guarded from the knowledge of associate spirits than their being thus conjoint with a man, for if they knew it they would speak to him, with the intention to destroy him. . . .'

'The delight of hell is to do evil to man, and to hasten his eternal ruin.'

A long note, written with a very sharp and fine pencil, in Mr Jennings' neat hand, at the foot of the page, caught my eye. Expecting his criticism upon the text, I read a word or two, and stopped, for it was something quite different, and began with these words, *Deus misereatur mei* – 'May God compassionate me.' Thus warned of its private nature, I averted my eyes, and shut the book, replacing all the volumes as I had found them, except one which interested me, and in which, as men studious and solitary in their habits will do, I grew so absorbed as to take no cognisance of the outer world, nor to remember where I was.

I was reading some pages which refer to 'representatives' and 'correspondents,' in the technical language of Swedenborg, and had arrived at a passage, the substance of which is, that evil spirits, when seen by other eyes than those of their infernal associates, present themselves, by 'correspondence,' in the shape of the beast *(fera)* which represents their particular lust and life, in aspect direful and atrocious. This is a long passage, and particularises a number of those bestial forms.

4.

Four Eyes were Reading the Passage

I was running the head of my pencil-case along the line as I read it, and something caused me to raise my eyes.

Directly before me was one of the mirrors I have

mentioned, in which I saw reflected the tall shape of my friend, Mr Jennings, leaning over my shoulder, and reading the page at which I was busy, and with a face so dark and wild that I should hardly have known him.

I turned and rose. He stood erect also, and with an effort laughed a little, saying:

'I came in and asked you how you did, but without succeeding in awaking you from your book; so I could not restrain my curiosity, and very impertinently, I'm afraid, peeped over your shoulder. This is not the first time of looking into those pages. You have looked into Swedenborg, no doubt, long ago?'

'Oh dear, yes! I owe Swedenborg a great deal; you will discover traces of him in the little book on Metaphysical Medicine, which you were so good as to remember.'

Although my friend affected a gaiety of manner, there was a slight flush in his face, and I could perceive that he was inwardly much perturbed.

'I'm scarcely yet qualified, I know so little of Swedenborg. I've only had them a fortnight,' he answered, 'and I think they are rather likely to make a solitary man nervous – that is, judging from the very little I have read – I don't say that they have made me so,' he laughed; 'and I'm so very much obliged for the book. I hope you got my note?'

I made all proper acknowledgments and modest disclaimers.

'I never read a book that I go with, so entirely, as that of yours,' he continued. 'I saw at once there is more in it than is quite unfolded. Do you know Dr Harley?' he asked, rather abruptly.

In passing, the editor remarks that the physician here named was one of the most eminent who had ever practised in England.

I did, having had letters to him, and had experienced from him great courtesy and considerable assistance during my visit to England.

'I think that man one of the very greatest fools I ever met in my life,' said Mr Jennings.

This was the first time I had ever heard him say a sharp thing of anybody, and such a term applied to so high a name a little startled me.

'Really! and in what way?' I asked.

'In his profession,' he answered.

I smiled.

'I mean this,' he said: 'he seems to me, one half, blind – I mean one half of all he looks at is dark – preternaturally bright and vivid all the rest; and the worst of it is, it seems *wilful*. I can't get him – I mean he won't – I've had some experience of him as a physician, but I look on him as, in that sense, no better than a paralytic mind, an intellect half dead. I'll tell you – I know I shall some time – all about it,' he said, with a little agitation. 'You stay some months longer in England. If I should be out of town during your stay for a little time, would you allow me to trouble you with a letter?'

'I should be only too happy,' I assured him.

'Very good of you. I am so utterly dissatisfied with Harley.'

'A little leaning to the materialistic school,' I said.

'A *mere* materialist,' he corrected me; 'you can't think how that sort of thing worries one who knows better. You won't tell any one – any of my friends you know – that I am hippish; now, for instance, no one knows – not even Lady Mary – that I have seen Dr Harley, or any other doctor. So pray don't mention it; and, if I should have any threatening of an attack, you'll kindly let me write, or, should I be in town, have a little talk with you.'

I was full of conjecture, and unconsciously I found I had fixed my eyes gravely on him, for he lowered his for a moment, and he said:

'I see you think I might as well tell you now, or else you are forming a conjecture; but you may as well give it up. If you were guessing all the rest of your life, you will never hit on it.'

He shook his head smiling, and over that wintry sunshine a black cloud suddenly came down, and he drew his breath in, through his teeth as men do in pain.

'Sorry, of course, to learn that you apprehend occasion to consult any of us; but, command me when and how you like, and I need not assure you that your confidence is sacred.'

He then talked of quite other things, and in a comparatively cheerful way and after a little time, I took my leave.

5.

Dr Hesselius is Summoned to Richmond

We parted cheerfully, but he was not cheerful, nor was I. There are certain expressions of that powerful

THE HOURS AFTER MIDNIGHT

organ of spirit – the human face – which, although I have seen them often, and possess a doctor's nerve, yet disturb me profoundly. One look of Mr Jennings haunted me. It had seized my imagination with so dismal a power that I changed my plans for the evening, and went to the opera, feeling that I wanted a change of ideas.

I heard nothing of or from him for two or three days, when a note in his hand reached me. It was cheerful, and full of hope. He said that he had been for some little time so much better – quite well, in fact – that he was going to make a little experiment, and run down for a month or so to his parish, to try whether a little work might not quite set him up. There was in it a fervent religious expression of gratitude for his restoration, as he now almost hoped he might call it.

A day or two later I saw Lady Mary, who repeated what his note had announced, and told me that he was actually in Warwickshire, having resumed his clerical duties at Kenlis; and she added, 'I begin to think that he is really perfectly well, and that there never was anything the matter, more than nerves and fancy; we are all nervous, but I fancy there is nothing like a little hard work for that kind of weakness, and he has made up his mind to try it. I should not be surprised if he did not come back for a year.'

Notwithstanding all this confidence, only two days later I had this note, dated from his house off Piccadilly:

DEAR SIR, I have returned disappointed. If I should

feel at all able to see you, I shall write to ask you kindly to call. At present, I am too low, and, in fact, simply unable to say all I wish to say. Pray don't mention my name to my friends. I can see no one. By-and-by, please God, you shall hear from me. I mean to take a run into Shropshire, where some of my people are. God bless you! May we, on my return, meet more happily than I can now write.

About a week after this I saw Lady Mary at her own house, the last person, she said, left in town, and just on the wing for Brighton, for the London season was quite over. She told me that she had heard from Mr Jennings' niece, Martha, in Shropshire. There was nothing to be gathered from her letter, more than that he was low and nervous. In those words, of which healthy people think so lightly, what a world of suffering is sometimes hidden!

Nearly five weeks had passed without any further news of Mr Jennings. At the end of that time I received a note from him. He wrote:

'I have been in the country, and have had change of air, change of scene, change of faces, change of everything – and in everything – but *myself*. I have made up my mind, so far as the most irresolute creature on earth can do it, to tell my case fully to you. If your engagements will permit, pray come to me to-day, to-morrow, or the next day; but, pray defer as little as possible. You know not how much I need help. I have a quiet house at Richmond, where I now am. Perhaps you can manage to come to dinner, or to luncheon, or even to tea. You shall have no trouble in finding me out. The servant at Blank

Street, who takes this note, will have a carriage at your door at any hour you please; and I am always to be found. You will say that I ought not to be alone. I have tried everything. Come and see.'

I called up the servant, and decided on going out the same evening, which accordingly I did.

He would have been much better in a lodging-house, or hotel, I thought, as I drove up through a short double row of sombre elms to a very old-fashioned brick house, darkened by the foliage of these trees, which overtopped, and nearly surrounded it. It was a perverse choice, for nothing could be imagined more triste and silent. The house, I found, belonged to him. He had stayed for a day or two in town, and, finding it for some cause insupportable, had come out here, probably because being furnished and his own, he was relieved of the thought and delay of selection, by coming here.

The sun had already set, and the red reflected light of the western sky illuminated the scene with the peculiar effect with which we are all familiar. The hall seemed very dark, but, getting to the back drawing-room, whose windows command the west, I was again in the same dusky light.

I sat down, looking out upon the richly-wooded landscape that glowed in the grand and melancholy light which was every moment fading. The corners of the room were already dark; all was growing dim, and the gloom was insensibly toning my mind, already prepared for what was sinister. I was waiting alone for his arrival, which soon took place. The door communicating with the front room opened, and the tall figure of Mr Jennings, faintly seen in the ruddy twilight, came, with quiet stealthy steps, into the room.

We shook hands, and, taking a chair to the window, where there was still light enough to enable us to see each other's faces, he sat down beside me, and, placing his hand upon my arm, with scarcely a word of preface began his narrative.

6.

How Mr Jennings Met his Companion

The faint glow of the west, the pomp of the then lonely woods of Richmond, were before us, behind and about us the darkening room, and on the stony face of the sufferer – for the character of his face, though still gentle and sweet, was changed – rested that dim, odd glow which seems to descend and produce, where it touches, lights, sudden though faint, which are lost, almost without gradation, in darkness. The silence, too, was utter: not a distant wheel, or bark, or whistle from without; and within the depressing stillness of an invalid bachelor's house.

I guessed well the nature, though not even vaguely the particulars of the revelations I was about to reveive, from that fixed face of suffering that so oddly flushed stood out, like a portrait of Schalken's, before its background of darkness.

'It began,' he said, 'on the 15th of October, three years and eleven weeks ago, and two days – I keep very accurate count, for every day is torment. If I leave anywhere a chasm in my narrative tell me.

'About four years ago I began a work, which had cost me very much thought and reading. It was upon the religious metaphysics of the ancients.'

'I know,' said I, 'the actual religion of educated and thinking paganism, quite apart from symbolic worship? A wide and very interesting field.'

'Yes, but not good for the mind – the Christian mind, I mean. Paganism is all bound together in essential unity, and, with evil sympathy, their religion involves their art, and both their manners, and the subject is a degrading fascination and the Nemesis sure. God forgive me!

'I wrote a great deal; I wrote late at night. I was always thinking on the subject, walking about, wherever I was, everywhere. It thoroughly infected me. You are to remember that all the material ideas connected with it were more or less of the beautiful, the subject itself delightfully interesting, and I, then, without a care.'

He sighed heavily.

'I believe that every one who sets about writing in earnest does his work, as a friend of mine phrased it, *on* something – tea, or coffee, or tobacco. I suppose there is a material waste that must be hourly supplied in such occupations, or that we should grow too abstracted, and the mind, as it were, pass out of the body, unless it were reminded often enough of the connection by actual sensation. At all events, I felt the want, and I supplied it. Tea was my companion – at first the ordinary black tea, made in the usual way, not too strong: but I drank a good deal, and increased its strength as I went on. I never experienced an uncomfortable symptom from it.

I began to take a little green tea. I found the effect pleasanter, it cleared and intensified the power of thought so, I had come to take it frequently, but not stronger than one might take it for pleasure. I wrote a great deal out here, it was so quiet, and in this room. I used to sit up very late, and it became a habit with me to sip my tea – green tea – every now and then as my work proceeded. I had a little kettle on my table, that swung over a lamp, and made tea two or three times between eleven o'clock and two or three in the morning, my hours of going to bed.

'I used to go into town every day. I was not a monk, and, although I spent an hour or two in a library, hunting up authorities and looking out lights upon my theme, I was in no morbid state as far as I can judge. I met my friends pretty much as usual and enjoyed their society, and, on the whole, existence had never been, I think, so pleasant before.

'I had met with a man who had some odd old books, German editions in mediæval Latin, and I was only too happy to be permitted access to them. This obliging person's books were in the City, a very out-of-the-way part of it. I had rather out-stayed my intended hour, and, on coming out, seeing no cab near, I was tempted to get into the omnibus which used to drive past this house. It was darker than this by the time the 'bus had reached an old house, you may have remarked, with four poplars at each side of the door, and there the last passenger but myself got out. We drove along rather faster. It was twilight now. I leaned back in my corner next the door ruminating pleasantly.

'The interior of the omnibus was nearly dark. I had observed in the corner opposite to me at the other side, and at the end next the horses, two small circular reflections, as it seemed to me of a reddish light. They were about two inches apart, and about the size of those small brass buttons that yachting men used to put upon their jackets. I began to speculate, as listless men will, upon this trifle, as it seemed. From what centre did that faint but deep red light come, and from what – glass beads, buttons, toy decorations – was it reflected? We were lumbering along gently, having nearly a mile still to go. I had not solved the puzzle, and it became in another minute more odd, for these two luminous points, with a sudden jerk descended nearer and nearer the floor, keeping still their relative distance and horizontal position, and then, as suddenly they rose to the level of the seat on which I was sitting and I saw them no more.

'My curiosity was now really excited, and, before I had time to think, I saw again these two dull lamps, again together near the floor; again they disappeared, and again in their old corner I saw them.

'So, keeping my eyes upon them, I edged quietly up my own side, towards the end at which I still saw these tiny discs of red.

'There was very little light in the 'bus. It was nearly dark. I leaned forward to aid my endeavour to discover what these little circles really were. They shifted position a little as I did so. I began now to perceive an outline of something black, and I soon saw, with tolerable distinctness, the outline of a small black monkey, pushing its face forward in mimicry to

214

'. . . He had cut his throat with his razor . . .'

(see p. 232)

meet mine; those were its eyes, and I now dimly saw its teeth grinning at me.

'I drew back, not knowing whether it might not meditate a spring. I fancied that one of the passengers had forgot this ugly pet, and wishing to ascertain something of its temper, though not caring to trust my fingers to it, I poked my umbrella softly towards it. It remained immovable – up to it – *through* it! For through it, and back and forward it passed, without the slightest resistance.

'I can't, in the least, convey to you the kind of horror that I felt. When I had ascertained that the thing was an illusion, as I then supposed, there came a misgiving about myself and a terror that fascinated me in impotence to remove my gaze from the eyes of the brute for some moments. As I looked, it made a little skip back, quite into the corner, and I, in a panic found myself at the door, having put my head out, drawing deep breaths of the outer air, and staring at the lights and trees we were passing, too glad to reassure myself of reality.

'I stopped the 'bus and got out. I perceived the man look oddly at me as I paid him. I dare say there was something unusual in my looks and manner, for I had never felt so strangely before.'

7.

The Journey: First Stage

'When the omnibus drove on, and I was alone upon

the road, I looked carefully round to ascertain whether the monkey had followed me. To my indescribable relief I saw it nowhere. I can't describe easily what a shock I had received, and my sense of genuine gratitude on finding myself, as I supposed, quite rid of it.

'I had got out a little before we reached this house, two or three hundred steps. A brick wall runs along the footpath, and inside the wall is a hedge of yew, or some dark evergreen of that kind, and within that again the row of fine trees which you may have remarked as you came.

'This brick wall is about as high as my shoulder, and happening to raise my eyes I saw the monkey, with that stooping gait, on all fours, walking or creeping, close beside me, on top of the wall. I stopped, looking at it with a feeling of loathing and horror. As I stopped so did it. It sat up on the wall with its long hands on its knees looking at me. There was not light enough to see it much more than in outline, nor was it dark enough to bring the peculiar light of its eyes into strong relief. I still saw, however, that red foggy light plainly enough. It did not show its teeth, nor exhibit any sign of irritation, but seemed jaded and sulky, and was observing me steadily.

'I drew back into the middle of the road. It was an unconscious recoil, and there I stood, still looking at it; it did not move.

'With an instinctive determination to try something – anything, I turned about and walked briskly towards town with askance look, all the time, watching the movements of the beast. It crept swiftly

THE HOURS AFTER MIDNIGHT

along the wall, at exactly my pace.

'Where the wall ends, near the turn of the road, it came down, and with a wiry spring or two brought itself close to my feet, and continued to keep up with me, as I quickened my pace. It was at my left side, so close to my leg that I felt every moment as if I should tread upon it.

'The road was quite deserted and silent, and it was darker every moment. I stopped dismayed and bewildered, turning as I did so, the other way – I mean, towards this house, away from which I had been walking. When I stood still, the monkey drew back to a distance of, I suppose, about five or six yards, and remained stationary, watching me.

'I had been more agitated than I have said. I had read, of course, as everyone has, something about "spectral illusions", as you physicians term the phenomena of such cases. I considered my situation, and looked my misfortune in the face.

'These affections, I had read, are sometimes transitory and sometimes obstinate. I had read of cases in which the appearance, at first harmless, had, step by step, degenerated into something direful and insupportable, and ended by wearing its victim out. Still as I stood there, but for my bestial companion, quite alone, I tried to comfort myself by repeating again and again the assurance, "the thing is purely disease, a well-known physical affection, as distinctly as small-pox or neuralgia. Doctors are all agreed on that, philosophy demonstrates it. I must not be a fool. I've been sitting up too late, and I daresay my digestion is quite wrong, and, with God's help, I shall be all right, and this is but a symptom of nervous dyspepsia." Did I believe all this? Not one word of it, no more than any other miserable being ever did who is once seized and riveted in this satanic captivity. Against my convictions, I might say my knowledge, I was simply bullying myself into a false courage.

'I now walked homeward. I had only a few hundred yards to go. I had forced myself into a sort of resignation, but I had not got over the sickening shock and the flurry of the first certainty of my misfortune.

'I made up my mind to pass the night at home. The brute moved close beside me, and I fancied there was the sort of anxious drawing toward the house, which one sees in tired horses or dogs, sometimes as they come toward home.

'I was afraid to go into town. I was afraid of any one's seeing and recognizing me. I was conscious of an irrepressible agitation in my manner. Also, I was afraid of any violent change in my habits, such as going to a place of amusement, or walking from home in order to fatigue myself. At the hall door it waited till I mounted the steps, and when the door was opened entered with me.

'I drank no tea that night. I got cigars and some brandy-and-water. My idea was that I should act upon my material system, and by living for a while in sensation apart from thought, send myself forcibly, as it were, into a new groove. I came up here to this drawing-room. I sat just there. The monkey then got upon a small table that then stood *there*. It looked dazed and languid. An irrepressible uneasiness as to its movements kept my eyes always upon it. Its eyes were half closed, but I could see them glow. It was looking steadily at me. In all situations, at all hours, it is awake and looking at me. That never changes.

'I shall not continue in detail my narrative of this particular night. I shall describe, rather, the phenomena of the first year, which never varied, essentially. I shall describe the monkey as it appeared in daylight. In the dark, as you shall presently hear, there are pecularities. It is a small monkey, perfectly black. It had only one peculiarity – a character of malignity – unfathomable malignity. During the first year it looked sullen and sick. But this character of intense malice and vigilance was always underlying that surly languor. During all that time it acted as if on a plan of giving me as little trouble as was consistent with watching me. Its eyes were never off me. I have never lost sight of it, except in my sleep, light or dark, day or night, since it came here, excepting when it withdraws for some weeks at a time, unaccountably.

'In total dark it is visible as in daylight. I do not mean merely its eyes. It is *all* visible distinctly in a halo that resembles a glow of red embers, and which accompanies it in all its movements.

'When it leaves me for a time, it is always at night, in the dark, and in the same way. It grows at first uneasy, and then furious, and then advances towards me, grinning and shaking, its paws clenched, and, at the same time, there comes the appearance of fire in the grate. I never have any fire. I can't sleep in the room where there is any, and it draws nearer and nearer to the chimney, quivering, it seems, with rage, and when its fury rises to the highest pitch, it springs into the grate, and up the chimney, and I see it no more.

'When first this happened, I thought I was released. I was now a new man. A day passed – a night – and no return, and a blessed week – a week – another week. I was always on my knees, Dr Hesselius, always, thanking God and praying. A whole month passed of liberty, but on a sudden, it was with me again.'

8.

The Second Stage

'It was with me, and the malice which before was torpid under a sullen exterior, was now active. It was perfectly unchanged in every other respect. This new energy was apparent in its activity and its looks, and soon in other ways.

'For a time, you will understand, the change was shown only in an increased vivacity, and an air of menace, as if it were always brooding over some atrocious plan. Its eyes, as before, were never off me.'

'Is it here now?' I asked.

'No,' he replied, 'it has been absent exactly a fortnight and a day – fifteen days. It has sometimes been away so long as nearly two months, once for three. Its absence always exceeds a fortnight, although it may be but by a single day. Fifteen days having past since

I saw it last, it may return now at any moment.'

'Is its return,' I asked, 'accompanied by any peculiar manifestation?'

'Nothing – no,' he said. 'It is simply with me again. On lifting my eyes from a book, or turning my head, I see it, as usual, looking at me, and then it remains, as before, for its appointed time. I have never told so much and so minutely before to any one.'

I perceived that he was agitated, and looking like death, and he repeatedly applied his handkerchief to his forehead; I suggested that he might be tired, and told him that I would call, with pleasure, in the morning, but he said:

'No, if you don't mind hearing it all now. I have got so far, and I should prefer making one effort of it. When I spoke to Dr Harley, I had nothing like so much to tell. You are a philosophic physician. You give spirit its proper rank. If this thing is real–'

He paused looking at me with agitated inquiry.

'We can discuss it by-and-by, and very fully. I will give you all I think,' I answered, after an interval.

'Well – very well. If it is anything real, I say, it is prevailing, little by little, and drawing me more interiorly into hell. Optic nerves, he talked of. Ah! well – there are other nerves of communication. May God Almighty help me! You shall hear.

'Its power of action, I tell you, had increased. Its malice became, in a way aggressive. About two years ago, some questions that were pending between me and the bishop having been settled, I went down to my parish in Warwickshire, anxious to find occupation in my profession. I was not prepared for what happened, although I have since thought I might have apprehended something like it. The reason of my saying so is this– –'

He was beginning to speak with a great deal more effort and reluctance, and sighed often, and seemed at times nearly overcome. But at this time his manner was not agitated. It was more like that of a sinking patient, who has given himself up.

'Yes, but I will first tell you about Kenlis, my parish.

'It was with me when I left this place for Dawlbridge. It was my silent travelling companion, and it remained with me at the vicarage. When I entered on the discharge of my duties, another change took place. The thing exhibited an atrocious determination to thwart me. It was with me in the church – in the reading-desk – in the pulpit – within the communion rails. At last, it reached this extremity, that while I was reading to the congregation, it would spring upon the book and squat there, so that I was unable to see the page. This happened more than once.

'I left Dawlbridge for a time. I placed myself in Dr Harley's hands. I did everything he told me. He gave my case a great deal of thought. It interested him, I think. He seemed successful. For nearly three months I was perfectly free from a return. I began to think I was safe. With his full assent I returned to Dawlbridge.

'I travelled in a chaise. I was in good spirits. I was more – I was happy and grateful. I was returning, as I thought, delivered from a dreadful hallucination, to the scene of duties which I longed to enter upon. It was a beautiful sunny evening, everything looked serene and cheerful, and I was delighted. I remember looking out of the window to see the spire of my church at Kenlis among the trees, at the point where one has the earliest view of it. It is exactly where the little stream that bounds the parish passes under the road by a culvert, and where it emerges at the road-side, a stone with an old inscription is placed. As we passed this point, I drew my head in and sat down, and in the corner of the chaise was the monkey.

'For a moment I felt faint, and then quite wild with despair and horror. I called to the driver, and got out, and sat down at the road-side, and prayed to God silently for mercy. A despairing resignation super-vened. My companion was with me as I re-entered the vicarage. The same persecution followed. After a short struggle I submitted, and soon I left the place.

'I told you,' he said, 'that the beast has before this become in certain ways aggressive. I will explain a little. It seemed to be actuated by intense and increasing fury, whenever I said my prayers, or even meditated prayer. It amounted at last to a dreadful interruption. You will ask, how could a silent im-material phantom effect that? It was thus, whenever I meditated praying; it was always before me, and nearer and nearer.

'It used to spring on a table, on the back of a chair, on the chimney-piece, and slowly to swing itself from side to side, looking at me all the time. There is in its motion an indefinable power to dissipate thought, and to contract one's attention to that monotony,

till the ideas shrink, as it were, to a point, and at last
to nothing – and unless I had started up, and shook
off the catalepsy I have felt as if my mind were on the
point of losing itself. There are other ways,' he sighed
heavily; 'thus, for instance, while I pray with my eyes
closed, it comes closer and closer, and I see it. I know
it is not to be accounted for physically, but I do
actually see it, though my lids are closed, and so it
rocks my mind, as it were, and overpowers me, and
I am obliged to rise from my knees. If you had ever
yourself known this, you would be acquainted with
desperation.'

9.

The Third Stage

'I see, Dr Hesselius, that you don't lose one word of
my statement. I need not ask you to listen specially to
what I am now going to tell you. They talk of the
optic nerves, and of spectral illusions, as if the organ
of sight was the only point assailable by the influences
that have fastened upon me – I know better. For two
years in my direful case that limitation prevailed. But
as food is taken in softly at the lips, and then brought
under the teeth, as the tip of the little finger caught
in a mill crank will draw in the hand, and the arm,
and the whole body, so the miserable mortal who has
been once caught firmly by the end of the finest fibre
of his nerve, is drawn in and in, by the enormous
machinery of hell, until he is as I am. Yes, Doctor, as

I am, for a while I talk to you, and implore relief, I feel that my prayer is for the impossible, and my pleading with the inexorable.'

I endeavoured to calm his visibly increasing agitation, and told him that he must not despair.

While we talked the night had overtaken us. The filmy moonlight was wide over the scene which the window commanded, and I said:

'Perhaps you would prefer having candles. This light, you know, is odd. I should wish you, as much as possible, under your usual conditions while I make my diagnosis, shall I call it – otherwise I don't care.'

'All lights are the same to me,' he said; 'except when I read or write, I care not if night were perpetual. I am going to tell you what happened about a year ago. The thing began to speak to me.'

'Speak! How do you mean – speak as a man does, do you mean?'

'Yes; speak in words and consecutive sentences, with perfect coherence and articulation; but there is a peculiarity. It is not like the tone of a human voice. It is not by my ears it reaches me – it comes like a singing through my head.

'This faculty, the power of speaking to me, will be my undoing. It won't let me pray, it interrupts me with dreadful blasphemies. I dare not go on, I could not. Oh! Doctor, can the skill, and thought, and prayers of man avail me nothing!'

'You must promise me, my dear sir, not to trouble yourself with unnecessarily exciting thoughts; confine yourself strictly to the narrative of *facts;* and recollect, above all, that even if the thing that infests you be, you seem to suppose a reality with an actual independent life and will, yet it can have no power to hurt you, unless it be given from above: its access to your senses depends mainly upon your physical condition – this is, under God, your comfort and reliance: we are all alike environed. It is only that in your case, the *paries,* the veil of the flesh, the screen, is a little out of repair, and sights and sounds are transmitted. We must enter on a new course, sir, – be encouraged. I'll give to-night to the careful consideration of the whole case.'

'You are very good, sir; you think it worth trying, you don't give me quite up; but, sir, you don't know, it is gaining such an influence over me: it orders me about, it is such a tyrant, and I'm growing so helpless. May God deliver me!'

'It orders you about – of course you mean by speech?'

'Yes, yes; it is always urging me to crimes, to injure others, or myself. You see, Doctor, the situation is urgent, it is indeed. When I was in Shropshire, a few weeks ago' (Mr Jennings was speaking rapidly and trembling now, holding my arm with one hand, and looking in my face), 'I went out one day with a party of friends for a walk: my persecutor, I tell you, was with me at the time. I lagged behind the rest: the country near the Dee, you know, is beautiful. Our path happened to lie near a coal mine, and at the verge of the wood is a perpendicular shaft, they say, a hundred and fifty feet deep. My niece had remained behind with me – she knows, of course nothing of the nature of my sufferings. She knew, however, that

227

I had been ill, and was low, and she remained to prevent my being quite alone. As we loitered slowly on together, the brute that accompanied me was urging me to throw myself down the shaft.

'I tell you now – oh, sir, think of it! – the one consideration that saved me from that hideous death was the fear lest the shock of witnessing the occurrence should be too much for the poor girl. I asked her to go on and walk with her friends, saying that I could go no further. She made excuses, and the more I urged her the firmer she became. She looked doubtful and frightened. I suppose there was something in my looks or manner that alarmed her; but she would not go, and that literally saved me. You had no idea, sir, that a living man could be made so abject a slave of Satan,' he said, with a ghastly groan and a shudder.

There was a pause here, and I said, 'You *were* preserved nevertheless. It was the act of God. You are in His hands and in the power of no other being: be therefore confident for the future.'

10.

Home

I made him have candles lighted, and saw the room looking cheery and inhabited before I left him. I told him that he must regard his illness strictly as one dependent on physical, though *subtle* physical causes. I told him that he had evidence of God's care and love in the deliverance which he had just described,

228

and that I had perceived with pain that he seemed to regard its peculiar features as indicating that he had been delivered over to spiritual reprobation. Than such a conclusion nothing could be, I insisted, less warranted; and not only so, but more contrary to facts, as disclosed in his mysterious deliverance from that murderous influence during his Shropshire excursion. First, his niece had been retained by his side without his intending to keep her near him; and, secondly, there had been infused into his mind an irresistible repugnance to execute the dreadful suggestion in her presence.

As I reasoned this point with him, Mr Jennings wept. He seemed comforted. One promise I exacted, which was that should the monkey at any time return, I should be sent for immediately; and, repeating my assurance that I would give neither time nor thought to any other subject until I had thoroughly investigated his case, and that to-morrow he should hear the result, I took my leave.

Before getting into the carriage I told the servant that his master was far from well, and that he should make a point of frequently looking into his room.

My own arrangements I made with a view to being quite secure from interruption.

I merely called at my lodgings, and with a travelling-desk and carpet-bag, set off in a hackney-carriage for an inn about two miles out of town, called The Horns, a very quiet and comfortable house, with good thick walls. And there I resolved, without the possibility of intrusion or distraction, to devote some hours of the night, in my comfortable sitting-room, to Mr Jennings' case, and so much of the morning as it might require.

(There occurs here a careful note of Dr Hesselius' opinion upon the case, and of the habits, dietary, and medicines which he prescribed. It is curious – some persons would say mystical. But, on the whole, I doubt whether it would sufficiently interest a reader of the kind I am likely to meet with, to warrant its being here reprinted. The whole letter was plainly written at the inn where he had hid himself for the occasion. The next letter is dated from his town lodgings.)

I left town for the inn where I slept last night at half-past nine, and did not arrive at my room in town until one o'clock this afternoon. I found a letter in Mr Jennings' hand upon my table. It had not come by post, and, on inquiry, I learned that Mr Jennings' servant had brought it, and on learning that I was not to return until to-day, and that no one could tell him my address, he seemed very uncomfortable, and said his orders from his master were that he was not to return without an answer.

I opened the letter and read:

DEAR DR HESSELIUS.—It is here. You had not been an hour gone when it returned. It is speaking. It knows all that has happened. It knows everything – it knows you, and is frantic and atrocious. It reviles. I send you this. It knows every word I have written – I write. This I promised, and I therefore write, but I fear very confused, very incoherently. I am so interrupted, disturbed.

Ever yours, sincerely yours,
ROBERT LYNDER JENNINGS.

'When did this come?' I asked.

'About eleven last night: the man was here again, and has been here three times to-day. The last time is about an hour since.'

Thus answered, and with the notes I had made upon his case in my pocket, I was in a few minutes driving towards Richmond, to see Mr Jennings.

I by no means, as you perceive, despaired of Mr Jennings' case. He had himself remembered and applied, though quite in a mistaken way, the principle which I lay down in my Metaphysical Medicine, and which governs all such cases. I was about to apply it in earnest. I was profoundly interested, and very anxious to see and examine him while the 'enemy' was actually present.

I drove up to the sombre house, and ran up the steps, and knocked. The door, in a little time, was opened by a tall woman in black silk. She looked ill, and as if she had been crying. She curtseyed, and heard my question, but she did not answer. She turned her face away, extending her hand towards two men who were coming down-stairs; and thus having, as it were, tacitly made me over to them, she passed through a side-door hastily and shut it.

The man who was nearest the hall, I at once accosted, but being now close to him, I was shocked to see that both his hands were covered in blood.

I drew back a little, and the man, passing down-stairs, merely said in a low tone, 'Here's the servant, sir.'

The servant had stopped on the stairs, confounded and dumb at seeing me. He was rubbing his hands in a handkerchief, and it was steeped in blood.

'Jones, what is it? what has happened?' I asked, while a sickening suspicion overpowered me.

The man asked me to come up to the lobby. I was beside him in a moment, and, frowning and pallid, with contracted eyes, he told me the horror which I already half guessed.

His master had made away with himself.

I went upstairs with him to the room – what I saw there I won't tell you. He had cut his throat with his razor. It was a frightful gash. The two men had laid him on the bed, and composed his limbs. It had happened, as the immense pool of blood on the floor declared, at some distance between the bed and the window. There was carpet round his bed, and a carpet under his dressing-table, but none on the rest of the floor, for the man said he did not like a carpet on his bedroom. In this sombre and now terrible room, one of the great elms that darkened the house was slowly moving the shadow of one of its great boughs upon this dreadful floor.

I beckoned to the servant, and we went downstairs together. I turned off the hall into an old-fashioned panelled room, and there standing, I heard all the servant had to tell. It was not a great deal.

'I concluded, sir, from your words, and looks, sir, as you left last night, that you thought my master was seriously ill. I thought it might be that you were afraid of a fit, or something. So I attended very close to your directions. He sat up late, till past three o'clock. He was not writing or reading. He was talking a great deal to himself, but that was nothing unusual. At about that hour I assisted him to undress, and left him in his slippers and dressing-gown. I went back softly in about half-an-hour. He was in his bed, quite undressed, and a pair of candles lighted on the table beside his bed. He was leaning on his elbow, and looking out at the other side of the bed when I came in. I asked him if he wanted anything, and he said no.

'I don't know whether it was what you said to me, sir, or something a little unusual about him, but I was uneasy, uncommon uneasy about him last night.

'In another half hour, or it might be a little more, I went up again. I did not hear him talking as before. I opened the door a little. The candles were both out, which was not usual. I had a bedroom candle, and I let the light in, a little bit, looking softly round.

'I saw him sitting in that chair beside the dressing-table with his clothes on again. He turned round and looked at me. I thought it strange he should get up and dress, and put out the candles to sit in the dark, that way. But I only asked him again if I could do anything for him. He said no, rather sharp, I thought. I asked him if I might light the candles and he said, "Do as you like, Jones." So I lighted them, and I lingered about the room, and he said, "Tell me truth, Jones; why did you come again – you did not hear anyone cursing?" "No, sir," I said, wondering what he could mean.

' "No," said he, after me, "of course, no;" and I said to him, "Wouldn't it be well, sir, you went to bed? It's just five o'clock" ' and he said nothing, but, "Very likely; good-night, Jones." So I went, sir, but in less than an hour I came again. The door was fast, and he heard me, and called as I thought from the bed to know what I wanted, and he desired me not to disturb him again. I lay down and slept for a little.

'It must have been between six and seven when I went up again. The door was still fast, and he made no answer, so I did not like to disturb him, and thinking he was asleep, I left him till nine. It was his custom to ring when he wished me to come, and I had no particular hour for calling him. I tapped very gently, and getting no answer, I stayed away a good while, supposing he was getting some rest then. It was not till eleven o'clock I grew really uncomfortable about him – for at the latest he was never, that I could remember, later than half-past ten. I got no answer. I knocked and called, and still no answer. So not being able to force the door, I called Thomas from the stables, and together we forced it, and found him in the shocking way you saw.'

Jones had no more to tell. Poor Mr Jennings was very gentle, and very kind. All his people were fond of him. I could see that the servant was very much moved.

So, dejected and agitated, I passed from that terrible house, and its dark canopy of elms, and I hope I shall never see it more. While I write to you I feel like a man who has but half waked from a frightful and monotonous dream. My memory rejects the picture with incredulity and horror. Yet I know it is true. It is the story of the process of a poison, a poison which excites the reciprocal action of spirit and nerve, and paralyses the tissue that separates

234

those cognate functions of the senses, the external and the interior. Thus we find strange bed-fellows, and the mortal and immortal prematurely make acquaintance.

CONCLUSION

A word for those who suffer

My dear Van L—, you have suffered from an affection similar to that which I have just described. You twice complained of a return of it.

Who, under God, cured you? Your humble servant, Martin Hesselius. Let me rather adopt the more emphasised piety of a certain good old French surgeon of three hundred years ago: 'I treated, and God cured you.'

Come, my friend, you are not to be hippish, Let me tell you a fact.

I have met with, and treated, as my book shows, fifty-seven cases of this kind of vision, which I term indifferently 'sublimated,' 'precocious,' and 'interior.'

There is another class of affections which are truly termed – though commonly confounded with those which I describe — spectral illusions. These latter I look upon as being no less simply curable than a cold in the head or a trifling dyspepsia.

It is those which rank in the first category that test our promptitude of thought. Fifty-seven such cases have I encountered, neither more nor less. And in how many of these have I failed? In no one single instance.

There is no one affliction of mortality more easily and certainly reducible, with a little patience, and a rational confidence in the physician. With these simple conditions, I look upon the cure as absolutely certain.

You are to remember that I had not even commenced to treat Mr Jennings' case. I have not any doubt that I should have cured him perfectly in eighteen months, or possibly it might have extended to two years. Some cases are very rapidly curable, others extremely tedious. Every intelligent physician who will give thought and diligence to the task, will effect a cure.

You know my tract on The Cardinal Functions of the Brain. I there, by the evidence of innumerable facts, prove, as I think, the high probability of a circulation arterial and venous in its mechanism, through the nerves. Of this system, thus considered, the brain is the heart. The fluid, which is propagated hence through one class of nerves, returns in an altered state through another, and the nature of that fluid is spiritual, though not immaterial, any more than, as I before remarked, light or electricity are so.

By various abuses, among which the habitual use of such agents as green tea is one, this fluid may be affected as to its quality, but it is more frequently disturbed as to equilibrium. This fluid being that which we have in common with spirits, a congestion found upon the masses of brain or nerve, connected with the interior sense, forms a surface unduly exposed, on which disembodied spirits may operate: communication is thus more or less effectually established. Between this brain circulation and the heart circulation there is an intimate sympathy. The seat, or rather the instrument of exterior vision, is the eye. The seat of interior vision is the nervous tissue and brain, immediately about and above the eyebrow.

You remember how effectually I dissipated your pictures by the simple application of iced eau-de-cologne. Few cases, however, can be treated exactly alike with anything like rapid success. Cold acts powerfully as a repellant of the nervous fluid. Long enough continued it will even produce that permanent insensibility which we call numbness, and a little longer, muscular as well as sensational paralysis.

I have not, I repeat, the slightest doubt that I should have first dimmed and ultimately sealed that inner eye which Mr Jennings had inadvertently opened. The same senses are opened in delirium tremens, and entirely shut up again when the overaction of the cerebral heart, and the prodigious nervous congestions that attend it, are terminated by a decided change in the state of the body. It is by acting steadily upon the body, by a simple process, that this result is produced – and inevitably produced – I have never yet failed.

Poor Mr Jennings made away with himself. But that catastrophe was the result of a totally different malady, which, as it were, projected itself upon the disease which was established. His case was in the distinctive manner a complication, and the complaint under which he really succumbed, was a hereditary suicidal mania. Poor Mr Jennings I cannot call a patient of mine, for I had not even begun to treat his case, and he had not yet given me, I am convinced, his full and unreserved confidence. If the patient do not array himself on the side of the disease, his cure is certain.

Dickon the Devil

ABOUT THIRTY YEARS ago I was selected by two rich old maids to visit a property in that part of Lancashire which lies near the famous forest of Pendle, with which Mr Ainsworth's 'Lancashire Witches' has made us so pleasantly familiar. My business was to make partition of a small property, including a house and demesne, to which they had a long time before succeeded as co-heiresses.

The last forty miles of my journey I was obliged to post, chiefly by cross-roads, little known, and less frequented, and presenting scenery often extremely interesting and pretty. The picturesqueness of the landscape was enhanced by the season, the beginning of September, at which I was travelling.

I had never been in this part of the world before; I am told it is now a great deal less wild, and, consequently less beautiful.

At the inn where I had stopped for a relay of horses and some dinner – for it was then past five o'clock – I found the host, a hale old fellow of five-and-sixty, as he told me, a man of easy and garrulous benevolence, willing to accommodate his guests with any amount of talk, which the slightest tap sufficed to set flowing, on any subject you pleased.

I was curious to learn something about Barwyke, which was the name of the demesne and house I was going to. As there was no inn within some miles of it, I had written to the steward to put me up there, the best way he could, for a night.

The host of the Three Nuns, which was the sign under which he entertained wayfarers, had not a great deal to tell. It was twelve years, or more, since old

Squire Bowes died, and no one had lived in the Hall ever since, except the gardener and his wife.

'Tom Wyndsour will be as old a man as myself; but he's a bit taller, and not so much in flesh, quite,' said the fat innkeeper.

'But there were stories about the house,' I repeated, 'that they said, prevented tenants from coming into it?'

'Old wives' tales; many years ago, that will be, sir; I forget 'em; I forget 'em all. Oh yes, there always will be when a house is left so; foolish folk will always be talkin'; but I hadn't heard a word about it this twenty year.'

It was vain trying to pump him; the old landlord of the Three Nuns, for some reason, did not choose to tell tales of Barwyke Hall, if he really did, as I suspected, remember them.

I paid my reckoning, and resumed my journey, well pleased with the good cheer of the old-world inn, but a little disappointed.

We had been driving for more than an hour, when we began to cross a wild common; and I knew that, this passed, a quarter of an hour would bring me to the door of Barwyke Hall.

The peat and furze were pretty soon left behind; we were again in the wooded scenery that I enjoyed so much, so entirely natural and pretty, and so little disturbed by traffic of any kind. I was looking from the chaise-window, and soon detected the object of which, for some time, my eye had been in search. Barwyke Hall was a large, quaint house, of that cage-work fashion known as 'black-and-white', in

241

which the bars and angles of an oak framework contrast, black as ebony, with the white plaster that overspreads the masonry built into its interstices. The steep-roofed Elizabethan house stood in the midst of park-like grounds of no great extent, but rendered imposing by the noble stature of the old trees that now cast their lengthening shadows eastward over the sward, from the declining sun.

The park-wall was grey with age, and in many places laden with ivy. In deep grey shadow, that contrasted with the dim fires of evening reflected in the foliage above it, in a gentle hollow, stretched a lake that looked cold and black, and seemed, as it were, to skulk from observation with a guilty knowledge.

I had forgot that there was a lake at Barwyke, but the moment this caught my eye, like the cold polish of a snake in the shadow, my instinct seemed to recognise something dangerous, and I knew that the lake was connected, I could not remember how, with the story I had heard of this place in my boyhood.

I drove up a grass-grown avenue, under the boughs of those noble trees, whose foliage, dyed in autumnal red and yellow, returned the beams of the western sun gorgeously.

We drove up at the door. I got out, and had a good look at the front of the house; it was a large and melancholy mansion, with signs of long neglect upon it; great wooden shutters, in the old fashion, were barred, outside, across the windows; grass, and even nettles, were growing thick in the courtyard, and a thin moss streaked the timber beams; the plaster was discoloured by time and weather, and bore great russet and yellow stains. The gloom was increased by several grand old trees that crowded close about the house.

I mounted the steps, and looked around; the dark lake lay near me now, a little to the left. It was not large; it may have covered some ten or twelve acres; but it added to the melancholy of the scene. Near the centre of it was a small island, with two old ash trees leaning toward each other, their pensive images reflected in the stirless water. The only cheery influence was that the house and landscape were warmed with the ruddy western beams. I knocked, and my summons resounded hollow and ungenial in my ear; and the bell, from far away, returned a deep-mouthed and surly ring, as if it resented being roused from a score years' slumber.

A light-limbed, jolly-looking old fellow, in a barracan jacket and gaiters, with a smile of welcome, and a very sharp, red nose that seemed to promise good cheer, opened the door with a promptitude that indicated a hospitable expectation of my arrival.

There was but little light in the hall, and that little lost itself in the darkness in the background. It was very spacious and lofty, with a gallery running round it, which, when the door was open, was visible at two or three points. Almost in the dark my new acquaintance led me across this wide hall into the room destined for my reception. It was spacious, and wainscoted up to the ceiling. The furniture of this capacious chamber was old-fashioned and clumsy. There were curtains still to the windows and a piece of Turkey carpet lay upon the floor; those windows were two in number, looking out, through the trunks of the trees close to the house, upon the lake. It needed all the fire, and all the pleasant associations of my entertainer's red nose, to light up this melancholy chamber. A door at its farther end admitted to the room that was prepared for my sleeping apartment. It was wainscoted, like the other. It had a four-poster bed, with heavy tapestry curtains, and in other aspects was furnished in the same old-world and ponderous style as the other room. Its windows, like those of that apartment, looked out upon the house.

Sombre and sad as these rooms were, they were yet scrupulously clean. I had nothing to complain of; but the effect was rather disappointing. Having given some directions about supper – a pleasant incident to look forward to – and made a rapid toilet, I called on my friend with the gaiters and red nose (Tom Wyndsour) whose occupation was that of a 'bailiff', or under-steward, of the property, as we had still an hour or so of sun and twilight, in a walk over the grounds.

It was a sweet summer evening, and my guide, a hardy old fellow, strode at a pace that tasked me to keep up with.

Among clumps of trees at the northern boundary of the demesne we lighted upon a little antique parish church. I was looking down upon it, from an eminence, and the park-wall interposed; but a little way down was a stile affording access to the road, and by this we approached the iron gate of the churchyard. I saw the church door open; the sexton was replacing his pick, shovel and spade, with which he had just been digging a grave in the churchyard, in their little repository under the stone stair of the tower. He was a polite, shrewd little hunchback, who was very happy to show me over the church. Among the monuments was one that interested me; it was erected to commemorate the very Squire Bowes from whom my two old maids had inherited the house and estate of Barwyke. It spoke of him in terms of grandiloquent eulogy, and informed the Christian reader that he had died, in the bosom of the Church of England, at the age of seventy-one.

I read this inscription by the parting beams of the setting sun, which disappeared behind the horizon just as we passed out from under the porch.

'Twenty years since the Squire died,' said I, reflecting as I loitered still in the churchyard.

'Ay, sir, 'twill be twenty year the ninth o' last month.'

'And a very good old gentleman?'

'Good-natured enough, and an easy gentleman he was, sir; I don't think while he lived he ever hurt a fly,' acquiesced Tom Wyndsour. 'It ain't always easy sayin' what's in 'em though, and what they may take or turn to afterwards, and some o' them sort, I think, goes mad.'

'You don't think he was out of his mind?' I asked.

'He? La, no; not he, sir; a bit lazy, mayhap, like other old fellows; but he knew devilish well what he was about.'

Tom Wyndsour's accent was a little enigmatical; but, like old Squire Bowes, I was 'a bit lazy' that evening and asked no more questions about him.

We got over the stile upon the narrow road that skirts the churchyard. It is overhung by elms more than a hundred years old, and in the twilight, which now prevailed, was growing very dark. As side-by-side we walked along this road, hemmed in by two loose stone-like walls, something running towards us in a zig-zag line passed us at a wild pace, with a sound like a frightened laugh or a shudder, and I saw, as it passed, that it was a human figure. I may confess now, that I was a little startled. The dress of this figure was, in part, white: I know I mistook it at first for a white horse coming down the road at a gallop. Tom Wyndsour turned about and looked after the retreating figure.

'He'll be on his travels to-night,' he said, in a low tone. 'Easy served with a bed, *that* he be; six foot o' dry peat or heath, or a nook in a dry ditch. That lad hasn't slept once in a house this twenty year, and never will while grass grows.'

'Is he mad?' I asked.

'Something that way, sir; he's an idiot, an awpy; we call him "Dickon the devil", because the devil's almost the only word that's ever in his mouth.'

It struck me that this idiot was in some way connected with the story of old Squire Bowes.

'Queer things are told of him, I dare say?' I suggested.

'More or less, sir; more or less. Queer stories, some.'

'Twenty years since he slept in a house? That's about the time the Squire died,' I continued.

'So it will be, sir; and not very long after.'

246

'. . . The Squire came to the side of the bed, lifted the boy and carried him out . . .'

(see p. 253)

'You must tell me all about that, Tom, to-night, when I can hear it comfortably, after supper.'

Tom did not seem to like my invitation; and looking straight before him as we trudged on, he said,

'You see, sir, the house has been quiet, and nowt's been troubling folk inside the walls or out, all round the woods of Barwyke, this ten year or more; and my old woman, down there, is clear against talking about such matters, and thinks it best – and so do I – to let sleepin' dogs be.'

He dropped his voice towards the close of the sentence and nodded significantly.

We soon reached a point where he unlocked a wicket in the park wall, by which we entered the grounds of Barwyke once more.

The twilight deepening over the landscape, the huge and solemn trees, and the distant outline of the haunted house, exercised a sombre influence on me, which, together with the fatigue of a day of travel, and the brisk walk we had had, disinclined me to interrupt the silence in which my companion now indulged.

A certain air of comparative comfort, on our arrival, in great measure dissipated the gloom that was stealing over me. Although it was by no means a cold night, I was very glad to see some wood blazing in the grate, and a pair of candles aiding the light of the fire, made the room look cheerful. A small table, with a very white cloth, and preparations for supper, was also a very agreeable object.

I should have liked very well, under these influences, to have listened to Tom Wyndsour's story;

but after supper I grew too sleepy to attempt to lead him to the subject; and after yawning for a time, I found there was no use in contending against my drowsiness, so I betook myself to my bedroom, and by ten o'clock was fast asleep.

What interruption I experienced that night I shall tell you presently. It was not much, but it was very odd.

By next night I had completed my work at Barwyke. From early morning till then I was so incessantly occupied and hard-worked, that I had no time to think over the singular occurrence to which I have just referred. Behold me, however, at length once more seated at my little supper-table, having ended a comfortable meal. It had been a sultry day, and I had thrown one of the large windows up as high as it would go. I was sitting near it, with my brandy and water at my elbow, looking out into the dark. There was no moon, and the trees that are grouped about the house make the darkness round it supernaturally profound on such nights.

'Tom,' said I, so soon as the jug of hot punch I had supplied him with began to exercise its genial and communicative influence; 'you must tell me who beside your wife and you and myself slept in the house last night.'

Tom, sitting near the door, set down his tumbler, and looked at me askance, while you might count seven, without speaking a word.

'Who else in the house?' he repeated, very deliberately. 'Not a living soul, sir'; and he looked hard at me, still evidently expecting something more.

'That *is* very odd,' I said, returning his stare, and feeling really a little odd. 'You are sure you were not in my room last night?'

'Not till I came to call you, sir, this morning; *I* can make oath of that.'

'Well,' said I, 'there was some one there, *I* can make oath of that. I was so tired I could not make up my mind to get up; but I was wakened by a sound that I thought was some one flinging down the two tin boxes in which my papers were locked up violently on the floor. I heard a slow step on the ground and there was light in the room, although I remembered having put out my candle. I thought it must have been you, who had come in for my clothes, and upset the boxes by accident. Whoever it was, he went out and the light with him. I was about to settle down again, when the curtains being a little open at the foot of the bed, I saw a light on the wall opposite; such as a candle from outside would cast if the door were very cautiously opening. I started up in bed, drew the side curtain, and saw that the door *was* opening, and admitting light from outside. It is close, you know, to the head of the bed. A hand was holding on the edge of the door and pushing it open; not a bit like yours; a very singular hand. Let me look at yours.'

He extended it for my inspection.

'Oh, no; there's nothing wrong with your hand. This was differently shaped; fatter; and the middle finger was stunted, and shorter than the rest, looking as if it had once been broken, and the nail was crooked like a claw. I called out, "Who's there?" and the light and the hand were withdrawn, and I saw and heard no more of my visitor.'

'So sure as you're a living man, that was him!' exclaimed Tom Wyndsour, his very nose growing pale, and his eyes almost starting out of his head.

'Who?' I asked.

'Old Squire Bowes; 'twas *his* hand you saw; the Lord a' mercy on us!' answered Tom. 'The broken finger, and the nail bent back like a hoop. Well for you, sir, he didn't come back when you called, that time you came here about them Miss Dymock's business, and he never meant they should have a foot o' ground in Barwyke; and he was making a will to give it away quite different, when death took him short. He never was uncivil to no one, but he couldn't abide them ladies. My mind misgave me when I heard 'twas about their business you were coming; and now you see how it is; he'll be at his old tricks again!'

With some pressure and a little more punch, I induced Tom Wyndsour to explain his mysterious allusions by recounting the occurrences which followed the old Squire's death.

'Squire Bowes of Barwyke died without making a will, as you know,' said Tom. 'And all the folk round were sorry; that is to say, sir, as sorry as folk will be for an old man that has seen a long tale of years, and has no right to grumble that death has knocked an hour too soon at his door. The Squire was well liked; he was never in a passion, or said a hard word; and he would not hurt a fly; and that made what happened after his decease the more surprising.

251

'The first thing these ladies did, when they got the property, was to buy stock for the park.

'It was not wise, in any case, to graze the land on their own account. But they little knew all they had to contend with.

'Before long something went wrong with the cattle; first one, and then another, took sick and died, and so on, till the loss began to grow heavy. Then, queer stories, little by little, began to be told. It was said, first by one, then by another, that Squire Bowes was seen, about evening time, walking just as he used to do when he was alive, among the old trees, leaning on his stick; and, sometimes when he came up with the cattle, he would stop and lay his hand kindly like on the back of one of them; and that one was sure to fall sick next day, and die soon after.

'No one ever met him in the park, or in the woods, or ever saw him, except a good distance off. But they knew his gait and his figure well, and the clothes he used to wear; and they could tell the beast he laid his hand on by its colour – white, dun, or black; and that beast was sure to sicken and die. The neighbours grew shy of taking the path over the park; and no one liked to walk in the woods, or come inside the bounds of Barwyke: and the cattle went sickening and dying as before.

'At that time there was one Thomas Pyke; he had been a groom to the old Squire; and he was in care of the place, and was the only one that used to sleep in the house.

'Tom was vexed, hearing these stories, which he did not believe the half of 'em; and more special as he

252

could not get man or boy to herd the cattle; all being afeared. So he wrote to Matlock in Derbyshire, for his brother, Richard Pyke, a clever lad, and one that knew most o' the story of the old Squire walking.

'Dick came; and the cattle was better; folk said they could still see the old Squire, sometimes walking, as before in openings of the wood, with his stick in his hand; but he was shy of coming nigh the cattle, whatever his reason might be, since Dicken Pyke came; and he used to stand a long bit off, looking at them, with no more stir in him than a trunk o' one of the old trees, for an hour at a time, till the shape melted away, little by little, like the smoke of a fire that burns out.

'Tom Pyke and his brother Dickon, being the only living souls in the house, lay in the big bed in the servants' room, the house being fast barred and locked, one night in November.

'Tom was lying next the wall, and, he told me, as wide awake as ever he was at noonday. His brother Dickon lay outside, and was sound asleep.

'Well, as Tom lay thinking with his eyes turned towards the door, it opens slowly, and who should come in but old Squire Bowes, his face lookin' as dead as he was in his coffin.

'Tom's very breath left his body; he could not take his eyes off him; and he felt the hair rising up on his head.

'The Squire came to the side of the bed, and put his arms under Dickon, and lifted the boy – in a dead sleep all the time – and carried him out so, at the door.

253

'Such was the appearance, to Tom Pyke's eyes, and he was ready to swear to it, anywhere.

'When this happened, the light, wherever it came from, all on a sudden went out, and Tom could not see his own hand before him.

'More dead than alive, he lay till daylight.

'Sure enough his brother Dickon was gone. No sign of him could he discover about the house; and with some trouble he got a couple of the neighbours to help him to search the woods and grounds. Not a sign of him anywhere.

'At last one of them thought of the island in the lake; the little boat was moored to the old post at the water's edge. In they got, though with small hope of finding him there. Find him, nevertheless they did, sitting under the big ash tree, quite out of his wits, and to all their questions he answered nothing but one cry – "Bowes, the devil! See him; see him; Bowes, the devil!" An idiot they found him; and so he will be till God sets all things right. No one could ever get him to sleep under roof-tree more. He wanders from house to house while daylights lasts; and no one cares to lock the harmless creature in the workhouse. And folk would rather not meet him after nightfall, for they think where he is there may be worse things near.'

A silence followed Tom's story. He and I were alone in that large room; I was sitting near the open window, looking into the dark night air. I fancied I saw something white move across it; and I heard a sound like a low talking that swelled into a discordant shriek — 'Hoo-oo-oo! Bowes, the devil! Over your shoulder. Hoo-oo-oo!ha!ha!ha!' I started up, and saw, by the light of the candle with which Tom strode to the window, the wild eyes and blighted face of the idiot, as, with a sudden change of mood, he drew off, whispering and tittering to himself, and holding up his long fingers, and looking at the tips like a 'hand of glory'.

Tom pulled down the window. The story and its epilogue were over. I confess I was rather glad when I heard the sound of the horses' hoofs in the court-yard, a few minutes later; and still gladder when, having bidden Tom a kind farewell, I had left the neglected house of Barwyke a mile behind me.

Sources

The sources I have consulted in compiling this book include: *The Purcell Papers,* with a memoir by Alfred Perceval Graves (London, 1880); *Madam Crowl's Ghost and other Tales of Mystery,* edited by M R James (London, 1923); *Wilkie Collins, Le Fanu and Others* by S M Ellis (London, 1951); *Ignorant Essays* by Richard Dowling (London, 1887); *Who Done It?* by Ordean A Hagen (New York, 1969); *Memoir of the Le Fanu Family* by T P Le Fanu (Manchester, 1924); *Seventy Years of Irish Life* by William Le Fanu (London, 1894); *Joseph Sheridan Le Fanu: a Memorial Discourse* by T S C Dagg (Dublin, 1949); *Sheridan Le Fanu* by Nelson Browne (London, 1951); *The Living Novel* by V S Pritchett (London, 1964); *Best Ghost Stories of J S Le Fanu,* with an introduction by E F Bleiler (New York, 1964); *Uncle Silas* by J S Le Fanu, with an introduction by Elizabeth Bowen (London, 1947); *The House by the Churchyard* by J S Le Fanu, with an introduction by Elizabeth Bowen (New York, 1968); *Joseph Sheridan Le Fanu* by Michael H Begnal (Lewisburg, 1971); *Uncle Silas* by J S Le Fanu, with an introduction by Frederick Shroyer (New York, 1966); *Victorian Doctor* by T G Wilson (London, 1942); *A Biography of Dracula: the Life Story of Bram Stoker* by Harry Ludlam (London, 1962); *Jung Stillung: His Biography,* translated by R O Moon (London, 1938); *The Life and Works of Dr Justinus Kerner,* adapted from the German by Anna Mary Howitt Watts (London, 1883); *An Omnibus of Crime,* edited by Dorothy Sayers (New York, 1929); *Dublin 1660-1860* by Maurice Craig (Dublin, 1969). My thanks to the staffs of the Library of Trinity College, Dublin, and the Westminster Libraries, London, who helped me trace many of the above books and also the original magazines in which Le Fanu's work first appeared; to Mervyn Wall, who showed me over the Le Fanu house in Merrion Square; and to Tom Buggy, a Le Fanu enthusiast, for his helpful suggestions.